M000215565

Setting Out

初旅

Setting Out

The Education of Li-li

by **Tung Nien**

translated from the Chinese
by **Mike O'Connor**

Pleasure Boat Studio

SETTING OUT
The Education of Li-li

by Tung Nien

Translated from the Chinese
by Mike O'Connor

Pleasure Boat Studio

Copyright 1998 by Mike O'Connor
All rights reserved

Cover photograph by Steve Johnson
Calligraphy by Liu Ling-hui
Design and composition by Shannon Gentry
Author photo courtesy of Lien-ching

Published by Pleasure Boat Studio
802 East Sixth
Port Angeles • WA 98362

Tel-Fax: 1-888-810-5308
E-mail: pbstudio@pbstudio.com
URL: http://www.pbstudio.com

ISBN 0-9651413-3-0
LCCN 97-76162

Printed in the United States of America by Thomson-Shore
First Edition

Chinese edition, *Ch'u-lu,* originally published by
Mai-t'ien Publishing Company, Taipei, Taiwan

This translation is for
Liam and Abby,
just "setting out";

and for

Jack Willits, chief engineer,
who sailed to Keelung many times

Translator's Acknowledgments

I offer my heartfelt thanks to my friend Tung Nien in Taipei for the opportunity to render his work into English.

I also gratefully acknowledge the Council for Cultural Affairs, Executive Yuan, Taiwan, Republic of China, for sponsoring this translation by means of a grant award.

Thanks also to Empty Bowl, Port Townsend, Washington, for support in the formative stage of this project .

And to poet-journalist Bill Bridges in Indiana for the painstaking and instructive editing of my early English version; and to Pleasure Boat Studio's Jack Estes, Shannon Gentry, and Bill Slaughter for their labor and vision in bringing this work (and others of cross-culural interest) to English-language readers.

And thanks also to Morgan Hill's best reader, Christina McLennan, for her constructive criticism of the manuscript; to independent-scholar Hunter Golay for his generous and illuminating elaborations on points of Chinese grammar; to artist Steve Johnson for "the photograph worth numberless words"; and to Rick Vuylsteke for his keen insights of Taiwan.

And to my wife, Liu Ling-hui, for answering—whatever the circumstances, whatever the hour of day—so many questions of meaning.

Mike O'Connor
Port Townsend, Washington
January 28, 1998
Year of the Tiger

Introduction

Many people are concerned that the vibrancy of current-day Taiwan is masking its past. Virtually everyone knows about Asia's "little dragons"—Singapore, Hong Kong, South Korea, and Taiwan—those predominantly rural and poor economies that only a few decades after World War II were transformed into international trade powers. The extent of Taiwan's economic accomplishments, moving from a rural backwater in the 1950s to a global economic player in the 1990s, can take on visceral strength after even a single day walking around Taipei, the sprawling metropolitan capital near the northern tip of the island. The languid pace of rural society, governed by seasons and weather, has long since disappeared. Economic change has reshaped virtually every aspect of life. The children of the sixties—people like Li-li in this book by Tung Nien—have seen generations of change squeezed into less than a single lifetime, a pace so rapid that even recent decades seem distant and indistinct.

The Ta-an district of central Taipei, for instance, has been reborn each of the past four decades. In the early sixties, students walked south from Hoping East Road along the narrow footpaths dividing rice paddies in order to reach the basketball courts at National Taiwan University. In the seventies, the paddies disappeared, with single- and two-story buildings thrown up along the winding lanes that replaced many of the paths.

In the eighties, a few broad roads cut swaths through the district, and four-story buildings with shops crowding their ground floors soon lined these new routes. And the raw cement structures typical of the time, gray and patterned with streaks of dark mold, were replaced by buildings faced with small white tiles. The nineties saw these walk-ups replaced by high-rises, more expensively clad in brick-shaped tile of various colors, some faintly attractive. The side streets of the area also became jammed by bamboo scaffolding as the land was cleared of the few remaining single-family homes for new apartment buildings to accommodate the city's burgeoning population, a product of the island's rapid urbanization.

Today, Ta-an is bordered on the east side by the pillars of Taipei's rapid transit system winding between eighteen-story high-rises and on the south by a six-lane expressway not far from those old basketball courts. The occasionally deafening nighttime cicada serenades of the past have been replaced by a constant din from traffic, sidewalk hawkers, Karaoke bars, and countless restaurants and shops. It doesn't take long to understand why so many Taiwanese tourists to the United States find New York City one of the most comfortable places to visit. Like home, it is *re-nao,* "hot and noisy," day and night. Conventional wisdom holds that Taipei represents the future: It is exactly what most of the island's municipalities, from Keelung in the north to Kaohsiung in the south, will eventually look like. Many communities are already pale blueprints.

Characteristic of a global trade power, Taiwan has become aggressively international in outlook, and this influences every aspect of life. Industrial-strength consumerism, for instance. Most metropolitan shop owners wouldn't think of closing until ten o'clock at night, and a large portion stay open later. Shoppers can close a deal on jewelry, clothes, electronics, or an automobile at an hour when most Americans are channel surfing for the best late-night talk show.

A closer look at the products on offer also tells a lot about how Taiwan has changed. Not too long ago, the island was known as the knock-off capital of the world, with counterfeit goods piled high in shops and on the spread-out blankets of sidewalk vendors. Not now. The government has cracked down hard on such operations. Although pirating has not been eradicated—and the biggest offenders are now in upscale, high-tech information industry products—enforcement has improved markedly. It's no longer possible to build a personal library or a brand name designer wardrobe for a pittance. Just as use of the Internet has permeated all aspects of society, so has the desire to be at the cutting edge of international fashion. Moreover, as the love affair with international products has intensified—including, it should be said, the latest books (often in translation) from major world publishers—shoppers have become more interested in buying the real thing, be it clothes, cosmetics, or software. The watchword in local advertising, and in newspaper and magazine articles, is "value for money."

There is a Chinese saying that "If you haven't eaten there, you haven't been there." Food is much more than a daily essential, for Chinese love to eat and they have a rich tradition of superb cuisine to show for it. While the regional cooking of China remains popular, eating tastes are also changing fast, in part because the brisk pace of life makes it difficult to spend as much time preparing labor-intensive Chinese dishes. The alternatives, especially in Taipei, are especially broad, from Chinese-style restaurants and snack-food vendors to the major cuisines of the world. European, American, and even Middle Eastern menus are widely available and surprisingly authentic. Like Japanese, Taiwanese are particularly attracted to Italian dishes, and to American fast foods from pizza to hamburgers to Subway sandwiches. A few decades ago, it was almost impossible to find a cup of brewed coffee. With local coffee consumption almost outpacing tea drinking, that's ancient history.

And the long list of restrictions that used to constrain all aspects of life under martial law, before it was lifted in July 1987, is also ancient history. In but a single decade, Taiwan has demonstrated that Western values can also be Asian values: Democracy can work in an Asian society. Here are free elections, a vigorous multi-party system, popularly elected officials, and a burgeoning number of civic and lobbying organizations at all levels. Until a decade ago, for instance, government regulations strictly limited the number and activities of civic groups. Today, there are so many non-government organizations, from private neighborhood committees to island-wide conservation groups, that it is difficult to estimate their number.

People now take freedom of religion, assembly, and speech—and freedom after speech!—for granted. The changes haven't all come easily, and political institutions have yet to mature fully, but no one has been stood up against a wall to make the transformations happen. Interestingly, the same people who were leaders of the ruling party (and only legal party) during the martial law period have adjusted their attitudes to embrace full democracy, and they now work closely with former members of the opposition, many of whom had been jailed for political reasons. The main political parties still have differing views on many domestic and international policies, as well as the best ways to implement them, but negotiation and compromise are replacing confrontation and fisticuffs.

The changes of the past several decades have, of course, taken many forms beyond shopping, eating patterns, and adaptations of Western democratic forms. Limited natural resources have always required Taiwanese to look outward. The first steps away from dependence on agriculture were possible in the fifties when small factories around the island started producing low-quality, labor-intensive goods. Thirty years later, those factories had moved to mainland China, replaced locally by high-value OEM (original equipment manufacturer) production for some of the biggest brand name companies in the United States and Europe. Although high-tech OEM production has remained strong, Taiwan's future lies elsewhere. Services already dominate the economy, and both the public and private sectors expect the island's business to shift toward financial services, telecommunications, air transportation, shipping, manufacturing, and media.

These commercial sectors are a far cry from the stuffed animals and low-end sports shoes of the past—and even that past is predated by this marvelous story, *Setting Out: The Education of Li-li,* which captures life as it was in Taiwan just before economic development, urbanization, and internationalization changed forever the fabric of society.

It is easy to be nostalgic about the past, to whitewash memory in ways that leave only mellow recollections of the best of what has been lost. Tung Nien does not fall into this trap. Here is a captivating collage of events, conversations, and musings centered on the early stages of a boy's maturation. Attitudes toward self, family, school and community life, government, foreigners, and the environment are themes that ripple through these pages like the breeze over ripe rice paddies. The experience is not always refreshing: The balmy air is sometimes fetid with the aroma of human fertilizer. The author gives us Taiwan's past, warts and all. One is transported by these pages to a time that has extraordinary texture and reality, and one that is not distorted by this careful and sensitive translation from the original Chinese into English. After turning the last page, readers will see that contemporary Taiwanese life has indeed changed markedly, but also that some patterns have endured. The reader's sojourn in the sixties—and the thoughts of Li-li—brings the present into clearer focus. It is a trip well worth taking.

Richard R. Vuylsteke,
Senior Editor, *Free China Review*

SETTING OUT
The Education of Li-li

1

Birds Singing

My father doesn't like the school in town. He says that al-though it's important for kids to do well on their middle-school exams, it's better if a school offers music, art, physical education, and other subjects more in touch with Nature.

For this reason, I transferred to another school, out of town. My mother also changed schools, but she's a teacher.

Mother and I also moved to a new house. It's a large, empty house in the suburbs, a country house people aren't using just now. It's very near the sea, though not so near to school. It will take half an hour to walk to school. The public bus is faster, but Mother says the buses don't come very often.

Father says he can come to see us a lot. Sometimes—usually on Sundays—we go back to our house in town. I like living out here. There are lots of kids in the neighborhood, and we can run and play just about anywhere. I often hear birds singing, and in the morning, from within our courtyard, I've spotted a tree squirrel.

2

First Day

Today was the first day of school. We left very early and waited on the road for the public bus. After a while, we saw a whole bunch of kids walking to school. Mother said we should also walk.

We walked beside a small river (I don't know where it starts) that flows past the wall of a big factory. It flows slowly there. The level of the river is quite a way below the surface of the road, some-times about the height of one person and sometimes the height of two. It's hard to tell how wide the river is because there's so much tall razor grass[1] growing on the sandy shore. The river looks muddy and shallow. At one bend, it flows under a bridge, and then the road runs along the other side of the river. That's where the projects

1

start, row upon row stepping up the mountain slope. All the houses have black wooden walls and big black roof-tiles. Lots of kids were coming out of them as we went by.

The river flows along another section of road and enters a tunnel where the water runs fast and loud. Near this is a large factory gate, and outside the gate are railroad tracks. The road, after a railroad crossing, slowly gets steeper, leaving the tracks below and the river, below that. The banks of the river at this point have become mountain cliffs, and the river most of the time is hidden by woods or thick grass.

The road then passes through a city wall, like the ones in our history textbook, that kind of wall, and gradually goes downhill. Beneath the hill are other housing projects. We met more kids going to school and adults leaving for work. Here we left the road by going down some steps, crossed over the railroad tracks, followed along a small road with a low wall, and then walked over the river on a big wooden bridge. The school is in a hollow of the mountain.

3

Brain Training

In trying to keep this journal, I don't think it's possible to write down all the things that happen in a day. Mother says, "Without experience a person cannot acquire knowledge." I'm not clear about what she meant. I finally explained it to myself this way:

To gain knowledge, you should do many things yourself. Your eyes have to see many things, your ears have to do lots of listening, and both your mind and body need lots of exercise. You must read many books, see many sights, listen to others, and also listen to music, all kinds of sounds, and ideas. You want your intelligence to be refined, sensitive. I think this is what my mother meant.

Writing a diary or journal is very interesting, though writing for a long time really tires me. Mother says to think of it as a kind of brain training.

4

Important Points

There is no way I can write in today's journal all about yesterday or today. There are just too many things to write down each adequately. I wrote about things along the way to school the first day, but then I didn't have enough time to write about the things that happened at school the same day. There are too many things to write about each completely. Even to write about something completely can never really include everything.

Mother says writing about the important points is best. Important points carry the significance, she says. But what is it that has significance? To have significance is to have value or worth. I'm still not clear. In this world, except for money and happiness, what other things have value?

5

Good-bye, Teacher

My new school is very small. My old school had five classes for every grade. This one has only two classes for every grade, and a kindergarten. Today, what a coincidence! On the school grounds I met my old kindergarten teacher. She has also transferred to this school.

She said, "Aren't you Li-li? You've grown tall," and she patted my head.

I thought this was a good chance to say something to Teacher Hsiung, but I was too shy. Fortunately, at the moment when she was going to leave, I managed to say, "Good-bye, Teacher."

Broomsticks for Bats

Today is the weekend, Saturday, and the class leader asked us who wanted to stay after school[2] and play baseball. Mother said I could stay, but not too late because we would be returning to town to eat dinner with Father. Besides the class leader, all the others who stayed were from First Village. First Village is the closest housing project to the school.

The students in our school, in addition to the children of the Harbor Bureau employees, include those whose parents work at the nearby factory, and other kids who come from town. Every day when it's time to return home from school, everyone lines up on the road according to where they live and what grade they're in. The lowest-grade students of the Harbor Bureau families assemble in front and Third Village sixth graders go to the back. Then, the whole body of students leave the school, march over the bridge, and cross the railroad tracks, finally going up the steps to the road before scattering.

At an intersection, the Harbor Bureau students take a special Harbor Bureau bus. Students from town go to a public bus stop. First Village students quickly go into their lanes and alleys. Second and Third Village students walk home along the road.

There are two ball teams. The team leaders are both First Village middle-school students. They mix in the students from the upper grades.

The first time I played baseball, I couldn't catch and I couldn't hit the ball, but many of the other kids were just like me. The bats and balls are different from the ones at my old school. Here they use broomsticks for bats and small leather balls, and nobody has mitts.

Father has read my journal and is rather surprised.

"Where has he found the time to build such a large vocabulary?" he said. "And he's written such accurate descriptions."

Mother said, "He's already finished reading the sixty-volume *Children's Stories of the World* in addition to more than twenty books of biography."

How Long Can a Fish Live?

Father ate breakfast and then went out to see to business. He and a number of foreigners have business dealings together. In the afternoon he was in a big rush and went with a friend to the seaside to go fishing, driving a car to the Pacific Ocean.

One time I went with them. They used a spinning reel and rod to fish with. The sea is very deep and the fish big. If they hit the tide right, they can catch dozens of fish. Sometimes the fish are so big two people have to hold them up.

The father wore a sleeved shirt and short khaki pants, along with a light chocolate-brown beret. On his back was a bamboo basket and on his shoulder two fishing rods made of jointed bamboo. The slim ends of the poles reached high in the air and, responding to his gait, never ceased jiggling.

Li-li had to walk fast to keep his father in sight. On his back, Li-li carried a canteen and an acetylene lamp.

They came out of the village and, at the side of the surrounding road, slipped down to a hillside trail choked with weeds. They entered a barren, swampy place where there had been a small lake. A fertilizer factory—day after day, month after month—had dumped calcium carbide powder and coal fragments into it, submerging so much material that now all that remained of the lake was a little corner.

"I've already caught that kind of big dragonfly," Li-li said, staring at a pair of green dragonflies with blue abdomens and black tails.

"This morning I caught five, one female and four males. Some friends taught me how. I used a broomstick in the water grass and stunned a pair of them. Then I took the female dragonfly and tied it to a line to trick the three males. I saw one male dragonfly stick its tail on the female's head. Sometimes the female curved its tail upward to touch the male dragonfly's stomach. What was that all about?"

"Oh," his father said, "it was certainly about something."

The fierce heat of the sun had passed, and gradually the evening breeze cooled Li-li and his father. They went past another swampy area and, coming to a hillside, ascended the trail to a mountain road.

"You ought to learn a little something from the mountains and the sea," his father said.

"Sure, I hope to learn how to swim," Li-li said. "Many of my friends already can float and keep their heads above water."

"I mean...." His father hesitated, then said nothing.

Between the trees at the side of the road, a nearby village became visible. Li-li could pick out several children close to it playing under banyan trees. They were children just finished with their baths, wearing freshly washed, white cotton sweatshirts. Only in the places where the shadows of the dense trees and the red-brick farmhouses did not fall was he able to see their images darting to and fro. Amid the shrill, metallic singing of the cicadas in the trees, he could barely hear what he imagined was their loud, happy laughter.

Li-li lifted his face to try to locate those exciting cicadas.

"Cicadas only live ten days or so," his father said. "During summer or fall, they live about ten days."

"Oh, so they're crying?" Li-li said and stopped to stare at one snug to a tree trunk, energetically drumming its abdomen. Its shiny black carapace, transparent wings, and protective membranes gleamed in the last light of dusk.

"Heaven knows," his father said, shrugging his shoulders. "Perhaps they're singing."

"What about the dragonfly?"

"What about the dragonfly?"

"How long do dragonflies live?"

"About ten days in summer or fall," his father said. "They come from inside the ground and go back into it."

"My teacher says dragonflies come from water."

"Sure, the idea is the same, in the end. All things return to the earth," he said and began to stride away.

"Spirits can fly to heaven," Li-li said.

"That would be better," said his father, "because below the earth it's dark and cold."

From gaps in the forest, Li-li again looked down and saw the village. Since leaving it, they had climbed far up the road and halfway up the mountain. He could just make out the irregular roofline and *several threads of cook smoke.*

"You've fallen too far back," his father called.

Li-li reached back and tightened the canteen to his body. It was again like leaving home, having to keep hurrying his steps to catch up to his father. At this moment, there was already a mist and gloominess settling over the trees. They hurried through another stretch of road, then climbed a flight of steps and came out of the woods.

"The weather is perfect," his father said, standing on the mountaintop. Lingering there, he took another look around, then slipped away down the green meandering slope.

The sea lay below the cliff face. The vast evening tide made a low thunder as it washed upon the sandy beach. In the harbor, fishing boats could be heard starting up, and the stacks of the boat exhausts, rising and falling with the waves, droned monotonously. From some far place on land, the spiraling song of a cicada seemed like the last sigh of day.

Coming down the mountain slope, they cut sideways and crossed the level floor of a mountain valley, then took a trail from the opposite mountain slope that fell to the beach beneath the mountain cliffs.

Wave after wave of the tide washed up bubbles of white foam on the sand. On the surface of the sea, the vivid wakes of fishing boats interlocked one after another. It wasn't long before Li-li and his father, walking along the beach, passed by a small fishing village and a grassy area with patches of yellow flowers. The swell of the sea suddenly fell quiet, and the sky's last colored clouds disappeared, one by one, in the night.

Finally, they scrambled over a flat stone slab and stepped up on a rock that jutted out to sea. A small boy waiting on the top hesitated to see who it was.

"Are you Mr. Li?" he asked.

"Yes," the father answered, "and you?"

"My grandfather is sick," the child said a little shyly. "I'll give you a boat to row."

"First let me thank you," the father said. "What's wrong with your grandfather?"

"Too old."

At the edge of the rock, the boy jumped to a high reef and, pulling firmly and steadily on a rope, towed a sampan near to shore.

"Today let me row," the father said, stuffing a bank note into the boy's pocket. "This evening I suddenly feel like rowing. You get in first."

"I can row," the boy said, his face reddening. "I row all the time."

"I know," the father said, "I can see you're strong. Next time for sure I'll let you row, okay?"

They left the shore. The sky was already completely dark, and they floated out under the glittering stars. The lights of the fishing boats shimmered everywhere in the dark sea.

The fisherman's son had his back to the sea and sat in the bow of the boat on a three-cornered board. Li-li sat on the cross seat in the middle of the boat. The two boys faced each other. In the stern, the father rowed and watched the peaks blacken and the mountain folds becoming more distant. The lighted village was surrounded by darkness.

"Why can't we see the moon tonight?" asked Li-li.

"The moon doesn't rise this evening," said the boy. "Tomorrow at dawn you can see it, one small part in the western sky. But you can only see it a moment before it sets in the sea."

"How do you know that?" asked Li-li surprised.

"Every day I watch," the boy said. Becoming animated, he hurried to explain. "The day after tomorrow, the morning moon will be bigger than tomorrow's, and it will stay in the sky a little longer because when it appears it will be higher and its shape will be changed a little. Finally, there's the day that, after the sun sets in the sea, we can see the full moon in the sky."

"Really?" said Li-li, turning to his father. "Is that the truth, Father?"

"Yes, it is," said his father. "He's a smart boy." Then Li-li's father said, "Later, the place where the moon appears each day moves eastward a little, and the moon becomes a little smaller, until finally it can't be seen anymore. Is that right, boy?"

"Yes, that's how it is," said the boy.

"It's very interesting," said Li-li, gazing into the night sky.

"You ought to learn something from the mountains and the sea," his father said.

"How long can a fish live?" Li-li asked.

The boy blinked.

8

"How long can what live?" the father asked, leaving off rowing. "What are you asking?"

"A fish, how long can a fish live?"

"How can anyone know that?"

"Their life…how long?"

The father thought a moment, then said, "If it comes to shore by being hooked, it can only live a few minutes; if it stays in the sea…." He shrugged his shoulders. "It all depends on fate. If another fish doesn't eat it, it can live for a while…a while longer." He fell silent a moment, then again turned to his rowing, at the same time muttering to himself.

"You must be rich people," declared the boy.

"What do you call `rich people'?" said Li-li.

"What you want, you can have," said the boy. "You get to study at school. I can't study anymore."

"Why can't you?"

"I can't study again," said the boy, "but some day I will certainly be a captain of a boat."

"I believe you will," said the father. "You know a lot about the sky and the sea. I'm sure someday you will captain a boat."

"I hope to travel very far," the boy said with enthusiasm. "Far, far from this shore," he added happily.

They were far from the shore now and the mountains were completely swallowed by darkness.

"Is this far enough?" asked the father. "This should be a good place to drop our lines."

"Row a bit more," the boy said with determination. "I know a good place."

Gazing into the black and mysterious depths of the sea, Li-li began to feel dizzy. "Can we turn on our lamp?" he asked.

"For the moment, we don't need a lamp," the father said.

"In a while we'll need one," the boy said. "I really have a good one."

"I have a lamp too," said Li-li.

"What kind do you have?" asked the boy.

"It's made of bullet metal," said Li-li pulling out a delicately shaped acetylene lamp. "The top layer holds the water, and the bottom *the carbide battery."*

"I know the kind, but it's too small," the boy said. "I use a lead acid battery. My lamp can shine deeper into the sea."

"I can catch fish," said Li-li. "This evening we're going to catch fish, right, Father?"

"Perhaps," his father said. "How about you?" he asked the boy.

"I always catch fish," the boy said, and quickly added, "I know how to land them. I never go home empty-handed because I wait until I've caught something."

They finally stopped the sampan and turned on both the battery-powered and acetylene lamps to prepare the fishing tackle. The fisherman's son cast his line first, far out on the surface of the sea. The lead sinker dropped into the darkness, making a distinct, crisp sound. Later, Li-li and his father cast their lines. The boy fixed his lamp with its piercing beam to the steel tubing of the gunwale. The glass-like surface of the steel tubing instantly reflected the light into the sea water, creating exquisite, bright blue colors, making everyone feel warm and hopeful.

"This evening I will surely catch some fish," said the boy.

"Will we catch some, too, Father?" Li-li asked.

"That's hard to say. We don't always get what we want," his father said. "The sea is so big, and there's so much to learn."

8

China's Hope

Today is Monday of the second week of school. At the weekly student assembly, the principal made a speech. She said that we Chinese in the last one hundred years were oppressed by foreigners during the first generation, and by both the Japanese and the Communist Party during the second. The hopes of China are with us, the third generation, and we should strive to be strong.

She also told us that she is a former student of Beijing College and a student refugee.

I asked Mother what is a student refugee.

Mother said, "A student refugee is a person whose country has been defeated and whose home has been lost. Such an unfortunate person then flees alone to another country."

Poor Principal.

9

Oriole's Song

We sang a song to a piano accompaniment. The words were:

> Look! Spring is coming.
> Listen! Spring is coming; how sweet the oriole's song.
> Green murmuring water—a girl's delicate eyes.
> Blue flora on mountains—eyebrows lightly painted.
> The sea is deep and the rocks old; friendship
> is forever.

Our teacher said, "Our lives should be animated with the spirit of spring, and we should treasure our friends."

10

Like a Princess

Our class has forty-two students. I still don't know everyone. Some, however, are easy to remember.

The class leader, for example, is very small, but energetic. The whole day he never stops doing something. Everyone likes to play with him. He tells funny stories, and his homework is especially good. He gets perfect scores in every subject and always ranks number one.

Chen Hsiao-wei is the most beautiful girl in our class. She looks like a princess in a fairy tale. The girl students from the Harbor Bureau and First Village all look the neatest and prettiest—the boys also are neat and handsome. Their pressed school uniforms are spotless and dignified looking.

Many of my classmates wear patched clothing and worn-out shoes. Second and Third Villages even have kids who go barefoot to school.

One of my best friends here is Lin Te-sheng, a Hunanese.[3] He loves to eat hot pepper sauce.[4] When the food vendor sees him coming, he quickly hides all the pepper sauce he has on hand because he knows Te-sheng can eat half a jar in one gulp.

Our teacher pays more attention to students from the Harbor Bureau and First Village. Our teacher also treats me very well.

11

Above the Cliffs

This morning in third period, first, second, and third grades were given a recess. Teachers from each of these grades, as well as some other teachers with special duties, took us to see a big ship enter the harbor.

We followed the small road by the side of the school up the mountain. It wound around and around. Sometimes we followed a big mountain cliff, and at other times we found ourselves in thick groves of trees. On the road, where the sky was blocked by the trees, two male teachers carried long bamboo poles to guide us. The first-grade teacher of A-class led us in singing a song. This school really likes to sing.

While walking along the road, we heard birds singing and saw all kinds hopping and flying about, catching the rays of the sun as they darted through the leaves of the trees. We also saw a group of mountain deer, which huddled among the dense trees and stole glances at us. One classmate threw a rock and scared them away. Our teacher struck the student across the palm, which he really deserved. There was also a kind of small, tree-trunk-climbing lizard. It looked scary. On the road lots of fallen leaves were stirring. Here and there we spotted bean-shaped droppings of sheep, but we didn't see any sheep. We sang songs and after a while reached the mountaintop.

From the top, we could see the ocean beyond Keelung Harbor.[5] Our teacher showed us where there had once been a Dutch fort, but now, except for a little bit of the foundation and remnants of the gun batteries, there is nothing left.

This was my first time to stand above the cliffs and see the ocean. It was also the first time that I saw a ship enter the harbor. To see the ship float up from the water's horizon was a real sight.

"The earth is round," said our teacher, raising his hand and making a fist. "Therefore, what we see first is the ship's mast."

12

Pens and Bookbags

Yang Te-chin lost a red Parker fountain pen that his mother gave him for his birthday. His mother is a nurse in the medical services office. After he told his mother, she reported it to our teacher. Our teacher was furious. During third period, our teacher wanted all of us students to leave the classroom and go out to the playground. The class leader inspected the book-bags of the row heads, and then the heads of each row inspected our book-bags. In all, they found four Parker fountain pens. Chao Han-sheng and I each have a blue Parker pen; Chen Shao-hui has a red one with her name engraved on it; and Lin Yu-ts'ai has a red pen without his name on it.

Our teacher wanted the two leaders to keep the matter a secret. However, someone told, and at noon, everyone was out playing except Lin Yu-ts'ai. He remained by himself in the classroom, standing and facing the wall in punishment.

Lin Yu-ts'ai insisted that the pen he had was the one his father had given him for his birthday, but no one believed this because his father is only a mine worker.

13

Dark and Light

Without light there is no object. In the dark, we cannot see any object. Form is produced by marking a borderline, but the borderline is only produced by the meeting of dark and light.

Between objects is always some distance. Also, every part of an object itself has spatial distance. That distance can be up, down, left, right, forward, or back. Every object has a part that can be seen and a part that cannot be seen. The part that can be seen is called the visible part. The part that cannot be seen can vary as much as our imagination allows.

This was the lecture in art class given by our fat teacher. He has long hair like a woman.

We painted three plaster objects—a sphere, a cube, and a pyramid.

14

Hold Tight to the Life Buoys

Yesterday at noon, Father left to go fishing. He said he wanted to catch the tide. A rising tide is easier to catch fish on. During ebb tide, the fish run to the deep ocean. Since Father was gone, Mother and I did not return to town this Sunday.

Mother bought some snacks and fruit, and also made a pot of beef stew. She brought along her students from Third Village to the seashore for a picnic.

Before there was any light in the sky, we went to see a fishing boat entering the harbor, and we bought several fish and squid.

Afterward, we passed by a sandy beach with big rocks on it, and from there watched the sunrise.

We used charcoal, dry wood and driftwood that had floated up on the shore. A bit to our surprise, we were able to make a breakfast of rice congee as well as a lunch. The weather was a little cool, but the fire pit and our playing kept us warm.

Everyone was happy playing on the beach, and we even collected some beautiful shells.

When it came time to part on the road home, the students hollered out, "Thank you, Teacher Lin."

Mother loves her students, but Mother loves me more.

They stood on the mountaintop looking far out to sea, reckoning the distance from the shore to Wild Willow Island.[6]

"It doesn't really look so far," said the boy who was the leader of the group. Although he was only an eighth grader, he already looked mature. He was wearing short red pants and had no shirt over his broad chest and muscular back. As he spoke, he looked down at the foot of the cliff, observing the rocks, reefs, and sandy beach.

The sun was still low in the sky as if it had not yet fully burned off the dawn chill. The surface of the sea was soft and pliant like a newly made bed. In the cool blue ocean sky, the black turtle-shaped island flashed in the light, a huge life-like animal facing out to sea.

"Li-li, do we really want to swim out in the sea together?" asked one of the younger children.

"We have a life buoy," returned Li-li. "If we hold tight to the life buoy, we'll be okay."

Then the group of boys broke off to go play baseball in a nearby field. They had a good time, making lots of noise, but not playing seriously. In the joy of the game, the ten or so friends forgot about age and grade. They needed to keep track of outs, but no one was keen on keeping score.

"Down the mountain!" the leader suddenly shouted. "Let's go down the mountain!"

On the steep mountain trail, they inched down the cliff. After a while, their bodies dripped with sweat and their limbs ached. By the time they reached the foot of the mountain, their faces were covered with dirt. The group—cheering, and without a moment's hesitation—raced down to the beach and jumped into the sea. The calm water where they leaped was transformed into foam and shouting.

"Li-li," the young boy asked again, "do we really want to swim with the others out to sea?"

"It'll be okay if you and I hold tight to the life buoys, like this," Li-li said, demonstrating to his small companion. He pressed the side of his face against the surface of his life buoy and made two vigorous kicks.

"If we do this, we can swim as far as we want," he added. "We just have to hold tight to the life buoy, like this."

"But I'll be scared. I really will be scared. Won't you?"

"I...if I were alone, I would be, but there are lots of us," Li-li said.

"Let's take advantage of the morning," the leader said. "When the sun gets high, it'll be too hot."

"Right," said another youth, who often served as the group's leader. "If we get too much sun, our shoulders will burn."

"You take the lead; I'll bring up the rear," said the leader. Then he turned to the others: "Let's go!"

The group surrounded the two small boys who clung to their life rings. At first, when the leg action of the two was still strong, the group could swim back or swim forward to catch hold of the life rings for a rest, or they could push the buoys like baby chairs to the forward-most point of the group. Later, the idea came to them of pushing the two life buoys in a competition. While this solved the problem of transporting the two small boys—neither of whom could swim—the farther the group swam, the greater became the problem of keeping everyone together. They became so carried away that in the resulting confusion they lost track of the leader.

"He and I were just now pushing Li-li," one boy said. "That was the last time we saw him. Right, Li-li? Right?"

"I don't remember," Li-li said. "He didn't push so often on this side of me."

"Right, right, the last time I was...we two together pushed Li-li."

"No," said the boy indicated by the other. "I just now and...and...somebody, somebody pushed Li-li. What a mess! We ought *to call for help, we ought to start yelling for help!"*

Some of the boys began to cry. They crowded together at the sides of the life buoys, their voices rising and falling as they shouted for help. But unable to bear their own pitiful cries, and choked in sobs, they stopped.

Li-li, holding firmly to the life buoy, looked from the group toward the distant shore. Some tiny figures on the beach were playing in the water. Near a curved reef, several fishing boats floated peacefully at anchor. The sun, shining brilliantly on the sandy beach, pricked the boys' eyes like a thin bayonet blade. A luxuriant grove of trees concealed dense vegetation and shadows. Beyond this, one person stood in the short brush behind several fishermen's wooden houses, apparently looking at something. He stood there, however, for only a moment, then vanished.

"No one has spotted us," Li-li said.

"It looks like someone has," one boy said, the muscles of his throat still contracting, unable to stop crying.

"Where? Where's the person you're talking about?" asked the youth who often served as leader.

"Behind the grove of trees. He's standing there watching us. He's been watching for a while."

"I can see him too, but I think he's only standing there to pee," Li-li said.

"Maybe he's going to get someone to rescue us."

But on the seashore there were no signs of activity, no people running out onto the beach waving handkerchiefs or clothing or anything to indicate alarm or rescue. The silence worried Li-li. Looking at the great broad wall of mountains behind the beach and the trees on the mountaintops, he imagined he could hear the sound of cicadas all along the high road.

"You probably saw a ghost," someone said impatiently. "Otherwise, why haven't we seen them?"

"Yes, we have surely run into a ghost," said another uneasy boy. "This surely has to do with ghosts."

This line of talk immediately made everyone more nervous. Submerged in the water, the dangling feet of the boys continued jerking to and fro in agitation. After a period of hesitation, some of the boys turned toward shore and swam off. Others first paused to consider the current and distance, then followed.

Li-li and his small companion were left alone. Right before their eyes they had seen the boys flee, waves of white foam trailing behind them.

"Are you going to leave me, Li-li?"

Gazing at his small companion's eyes full of tears, Li-li sighed deeply, swallowed a little water, and said, "I...I won't leave you; don't worry. We'll hold tight to the life buoys, like this. Come on, we'll get a little closer. Together we can swim and make headway."

"I can't move my feet."

"Relax a bit, then you can move them. Watch me." Li-li stretched out both feet behind him. He kicked and churned up some white water. But this demonstration didn't have much effect. Paralyzed with fear, the boy couldn't hold onto his life buoy any longer and slipped into the sea. He flailed his two arms at the surface of the water struggling to keep afloat, but he could not cry out. Every time that he fought his way up to the surface, he choked on more water. Finally, he was completely submerged, and his white body, seeming to melt like wax, disappeared into the sea without a trace.

Trembling with anxiety, Li-li sensed that his own two feet had become rigid like rocks. He crawled up on the life buoy and spread out his limbs to establish some stability. For a time, his face almost touched the surface of the water. His became afraid that from the calm of the sea a ring of water might suddenly rise up and swallow him, too. He watched the soft, noiseless surface as if it were a trap. But the sea water flowed peacefully toward shore, and he was gradually pushed forward.

As time passed, the tension in his body eased. His throat also felt less parched. At last, he ceased to be obsessed with signs from the sea. He remembered when the group of boys had stood on the rock cliff and looked out at the sea. Once this thought had struck him, he could not help but raise his lowered head from the life buoy and gradually, very carefully observe the great, broad surface of the sea. There, floating on the watery horizon, was the black island.

Watching awhile, he then tried using his two hands as oars. He paddled on the surface of the sea. "Thank heaven," he thought. "I'm making headway. I'm making headway."

15

Mother or Father

At some time past nine o'clock, Father came home with two fish. I had just finished my homework and was reading *The Count of Monte Cristo.*

Father came into my room and asked about school affairs. He said our student counselor is his old classmate. Our student counselor once told me this as well. Father, before leaving my room, looked through my journal. He suddenly asked, "Do you love your father or mother more?"

I had been absorbed in reading about the Count of Monte Cristo rowing on the sea in a boat and, not really thinking carefully, I said, "I love Mother more."

Father silently nodded his head a few times, then a moment later spoke again, "You ought to find time to learn the piano or to paint."

He's already told me this twice. It's clearly his hope for me, so I said, "Okay."

He patted my head and went out.

16

Wild Ox

A neighbor, and classmate of mine, was killed by an ox-drawn cart. He was crossing an avenue with his head down. The cart was on a hill carrying a big load of sand and dirt when the brakes went out. The ox ran wild and crashed into the boy, knocking him down. People in the area brought out grass mats to cover him with, but the blood wouldn't stop flowing.

17

Newspaper Scholars

Mother's subscription to the *United Daily News* finally begins today. In this neighborhood there are no other people who subscribe to a newspaper, so the newsboy didn't want to come here. He said that to deliver only one newspaper in this neighborhood was not profitable. In order to do the newsboy a favor, Mother also subscribed to the children's *National Language Daily*.[7]

I like to read the adult newspaper best. It has many strange stories and news reports. No wonder people say that by reading the newspaper, scholars can know the world's affairs without leaving their door.

Here are some things I read today:

*Around noon yesterday there was a motorized junk of the armed forces of the Republic of China heading for Matsu Island[8] when it was lost in a big fog. It met up with Communist bandit gunboats and was sunk in a surprise attack.

*This year primary schools in the whole province of Taiwan added 2,568 classes. In our city, Keelung, we added sixty-eight.

*In Mexico a big earthquake killed two thousand people and injured more than ten thousand.

18

Jump Rope

In gym class the teacher taught us how to jump rope. At first I could only jump seven or eight times in a row. But by the end of class, I could jump more than a hundred times.

At afternoon student-activity time, I went again up the backside of the mountain to gather botanical specimens. I don't know why this school, every day before letting out, always arranges such activities for us. Nevertheless, I love collecting botanical specimens. Maybe I'll become a botanist. However, this kind of activity is hard.

There are students who already can't stand it. They've switched to sports, chess, or choir, and such.

19

Mahler's Fifth

In the morning I felt too dizzy to get up. Mother said I had a fever. We called Father and he brought a doctor friend to see me. The doctor said I'd caught a cold, and he gave me a shot and some medicine. When I woke up, it was already afternoon. In the living room, Mahler's *Fifth Symphony* was playing on the phonograph, and Father was outside in the yard tending the lawn and flower garden.

"Last night when you were sleeping, you kicked the quilt off, didn't you?" Father said.

"I don't know. But yesterday, during gym class, I sweated a lot," I said.

"Your constitution isn't strong enough yet," Father said.

20

Wax Candles

After school on the way home, Mother bought two wax candles at the grocery store to use during electricity blackouts. The newspaper says that the blackouts will begin today throughout the island, alternating each day among districts.

Last year there were seven or eight floods. This year there's a drought. We haven't had any rain for several months. Sun Moon Lake's[9] waterline is not even twenty-nine centimeters, which nearly makes it impossible to generate electricity. No wonder that in the villages the wells for drinking water are drying up fast. Drinking water could become a problem very soon, though not for the neighboring Third Village, nor the Mining Village, where running-water facilities are taken care of by the government.

Keelung Harbor

On Sunday, Mother's class again had an outing. This time even more students joined in, and the trip was farther than the first one. She assembled the students from three villages along the road, and the students in dormitories of the Harbor Administration Bureau near Hsien Tung Yen[10] met up with them. That side is Keelung Harbor's northwest shore. We town families, and the train station as well, are on the south shore. I'm now starting to realize just how big Keelung Harbor really is.

Standing on the mountaintop and looking out at the harbor, Mother told us that the Spanish arrived there in 1626. On Peace Island they built the town of San Salvador, and at Tamsui they built the town of San Domingo. In this area, the Spanish and mainland Chinese, as well as the Japanese, carried on trade in deer hides and sulfur.

The Dutch also came to Keelung.

22

What Was That All About?

During afternoon free-activity time, while we played blindman's buff, Wang Chih-kuo saw a boy belonging to Mother's class writing his name and that of Chen Hsiao-wei—who is in our class—on the wooden wall of an old classroom. He carved his and her names on either side of a heart and in the center of the heart added the double *hsi* "word" for happiness twice over.[11]

That same wall follows a small ditch of water that runs out of a cleft in the mountain cliffs. It's very narrow between the ditch and the wall, and the smell's not so good. Still, many classmates ran by for a look, and the boys teased Chen Hsiao-wei, making her cry in anger.

Our teacher punished the boys, and later I told Mother the

story. After school on the way home, I asked, "What punishment will you give your student for carving on the wall?"

"Well, I can only punish him for defacing public property," Mother said and laughed. "Do you think I ought to punish him for something else?"

"He's girl crazy," I said. "There's lots of girls in his own class, but they're not enough for him. He loves to come to our class."

Out of doors in the rural air, the teacher played the accordion with expert ease. He customarily taught the children throughout the morning. Following the instrument's deep resonance, the chorus of voices sang and harmonized.

"You're half a beat fast," said the teacher, who was Li-li's uncle on his father's side,[12] stopping the accordion. With his honest plump face, he laughed and said, "Li-li, you're still half a beat fast. Why are you still fast?"

"Oh, I...I'm watching a little bird," Li-li said and blushed. "I see a little bird on the rooftop."

"All right, we'll start again from the beginning. Li-li, this time pay attention."

The accordion's sound began, embellished by the light caroling of the children and the small birds chirping and twittering. Li-li stood on a rung of a bamboo ladder which leaned against a high pile of rice straw. Standing there, he could see the rooftop on the back side of the traditional farmhouse with its three sides and inner courtyard. Sparrows in a small flock perched on the ridge of the roof using their claws to scratch, or whetted their beaks on the edges of the roof-tiles. Others hopped and flitted about, with sudden spurts of energy, or trailed along the slanted roof and swooped off the house.

Li-li was not really interested in the sparrows. Instead he focused on the face of a small sleeping girl within a small rectangular window of a thick wall. He could see the window through the leaves of a guava tree in the courtyard garden.

"You're singing very good, especially good. Let's sing another song," said Uncle. "Li-li, hey, Li-li, are you listening?"

"Uh, yes, I'm listening, I . . ."

"I see you're distracted, and where you're standing, by the way,

is dangerous," Uncle said, approaching the stack of rice straw and gripping the ladder to stabilize it. "Come down, before you fall down. That would be terrible."

"I'm not in danger," Li-li said, grasping the car tire that weighted the rice-straw pile and projected from the top. "See. I'm holding tight to this and there's no danger."

"It's still safer if you come down," the uncle said. "Otherwise you might stumble and crack your head; then you won't be able to sing anymore."

"Ha, ha," said Li-li's cousin.[13] "If he falls and knocks his mouth crooked, he also won't sing anymore."

Hesitating a moment, Li-li, turning red again, said, "I like standing here. I like standing here looking at the view. I came to the country to see the views. My mother wanted me to come to the country to see the scenery."

"All right," Uncle said. "But be careful. We'll begin singing another song. Li-li, do you know `White Jasmine'?"

Li-li quickly recited, "How beautiful a white jasmine."

"Good," Uncle said. Then, beginning to play the accordion, he added, "This is a song we have all learned."

Within that dim window, the small face of the sleeping girl lay on the pillow. It seemed to Li-li to be a face still pale with fear.

The first morning they met, Li-li noticed that her cheeks were like ripe peaches tinged with red. At that time, she stood behind her mother, grasping a fold of her mother's skirt, half covering her face. Her mother said, "Are you shy? He's your cousin.[14] When you both grow up, you will marry each other. You will be a daughter-in-law in their family."

"How beautiful a white jasmine." The happy singing of the small birds blended with the instrument's music. The sweet singing of the children continued: "How beautiful a white jasmine."

"Wake up!" Li-li softly cried in his heart. "Hurry and wake up!"

"Go play with your cousin," her mother said, leading the girl out from behind her. "Go with your cousin for a walk somewhere."

The morning sun, already above the ridge of the roof, was burn-

ing intensely in the backyard and on the low brick wall. "Better wear your hat," Li-li's aunt said, using her fingers to comb her daughter's long wavy hair, and then helping her put on a broad-brimmed straw hat. "Li-li, you're not wearing a hat?"

"I'm not afraid of the sun," Li-li said.

"You still ought to wear a hat," his aunt said. "If you sunburn, perhaps your little cousin won't love you."

"Okay," said Li-li, plucking the broad-brimmed bamboo hat off the low wall, "I'll wear this one."

They followed along the low wall and took a narrow path into the shade of the trees. Li-li's little cousin followed behind him. Several times she turned to look back at her mother. Finally, her mother went around the corner and disappeared. They came to a huge dry field that baked in the hot sun.

"Do you know what this is?" Li-li asked, pointing to a rice plant on the dried ground. There was no answer. He continued, "It's the root of a rice plant. I saw them cut the rice, and at first I thought that the plants were left behind to grow into new rice plants. But it's not so. They rot; then, after being trampled, they go into the soft mud and become fertilizer. Finally the farmers sow new plants and then transplant the rice seedlings. It's very interesting, don't you think?"

Li-li was half a head taller than her, and the brim of her hat obstructed her face. He thought she must be either gazing at the ruined standing rice plants, staring vacantly, or perhaps, gazing serenely far off at the wilderness landscape. He lowered his head to look at the side of her face and said, "Don't you want to say anything?" Her face blushed bright red; on the tip of her nose a few tiny beads of sweat appeared.

"This time I'll sing a song myself and you listen." Improvising and pressing a few keys, Uncle asked, "What song shall I sing?"

" 'Two Lao Ku,' "[15] said one child, striking the palms of his hands together. "Let us hear 'Two Lao Ku.'"

"Heh, heh. `Lao hu' has become `lau ku,'" said the uncle,

joining in with the laughter of the others. "This time I'll sing `O Sole Mio.'"

"What is `O Sole Mio'?"

"Lovely Sunshine," and so saying Uncle began to play the accordion. He enjoyed his own singing very much.

Leaning against the wooden wall of a godown,[16] they sat on the ground shoulder to shoulder in the shade of a longan tree[17] to rest. Earlier, near a private estate, they had seen a white-headed pig in a pigsty and a flock of hundreds of chickens in a chicken yard. Later, following along the stream bank in a bamboo grove, they had gathered brackens.

Li-li threw down his hat beside his heels in the grass. The girl held her broad hat properly on her knees against her chest. The sun illuminated a bluish-green patch of lush grass beyond the shade of the wall and the trees. There the morning dew was changing into a dim vapor. By the green border of the grass, dense hibiscus trees formed a hedge with red flower bunches and fresh, lovely yellow stamens. Beyond the hedge was an expanse of sky with a few white clouds.

"How peaceful," said Li-li. "Isn't it peaceful?"

Her mouth was still pursed, and she only turned to view the distant blue-green mountains. It was extremely quiet, and Li-li seemed able to hear only slight indistinct breathing. After just a moment, however, a trembling moan came from inside the godown. They turned around to a crack in the wall to look. In a patch of bright sunlight below a window, they saw Second Uncle naked below the waist pushing a woman down onto a heap of rice bags. The woman's clothes were strewn about, and neither her head nor face could be seen beneath his embrace. But her two hands, being used to ward off his chin, were visible. His knees held apart her cloud-white legs and his groin thrust forward a fleshy club that forcefully joined her body. Fresh blood appeared.

Li-li and his cousin, at the same time, turned away in shock from the crack in the wall. They looked fearfully at each other. Li-li saw the vivid redness draining from the face of his little cousin, and her shoulders tensed and trembled. Putting his index finger to his lips, he quietly said, "Don't be afraid. I'll protect you." He reached out both hands to hold her, but the sudden move frightened her.

"Mama," she cried trembling with fear, then turned and squirmed out of his embrace and ran off toward the village.

Li-li's chest again shook with apprehension, and his two trembling legs made the ladder wobble.

"You see, you see!" Uncle said, breaking off from his singing and going over to the stack of rice-straw to clutch the ladder, "You come down right now! Li-li, right now!" He turned to the other children and said, "All right, we have sung enough today; we can stop here. Everybody go now and wash up for lunch."

Again casting a last brief glance at the sleeping face in the window, Li-li, biting his lip, climbed down the ladder, tears welling in his eyes.

"What's the matter with you today?" Uncle asked, stroking Li-li's head.

"I saw Second Uncle take off a woman's clothes, and he pushed her down on a sack of rice. What was that all about?" Li-li asked.

"You saw this standing on the ladder?"

Shaking his head, Li-li said, "Outside the village in a godown."

"He loves her, certainly that's it."

"But, a...a...he made blood flow from her bottom, and he hurt her."

"Huh." The uncle was silent for a moment, then said, "Oh that's nothing. Your family's Second Uncle is a veterinarian. I'm sure that was blood from a chicken he killed."

"Oh," Li-li said, "Yes, but . . ."

"That was all it was. He's a vet for the Farmer's Association," Uncle said. "Don't think of it again. We'll take our afternoon nap and later sing some more good songs, okay?"

"That's right," Li-li said blinking. "He is a veterinarian."

23

French Horn

Today our music teacher introduced us to the French horn. He reminded us to pay attention to the music broadcast on the school grounds that has that BA, BA, BA-BA kind of horn sound.

Mother says that our record of Mozart's *French Concerto in D-Major* is at our home in town. Next time we go there we can get it.

Today we learned another new song:

I remember when we were young—
I loved to talk and you to laugh;
side by side under the pear tree—
wind in the branch tips,
the birds singing.
We never knew how we finally fell asleep,
but in our dreams the flowers fell.

24

President Chiang

In the morning meeting, the student counselor said that [18] President Chiang[19] yesterday afternoon came to Keelung Harbor. He was there to inspect an American nuclear submarine. The student counselor emphasized that President Chiang was an especially great man, and that we should support his continuing in office.

I also read about this in the newspaper. President Chiang boarded the submarine *Swordfish* for a three-and-a-half-hour inspection. He personally piloted the vessel for four hundred meters in the deep ocean, sailing for ten minutes.

I'd really love to steer such a boat if I were President Chiang. It'd be great. But if I were an orphan that would be good too because today Keelung Harbor has another American destroyer, and it will receive thirty orphans from the Nuannuan Po Ai Orphanage. The Americans invited the orphans aboard the ship to have lunch and see a movie. They will also be given toys and candy.

This same destroyer came to Taiwan bringing large contributions of clothing from the American people to refugees of our big flood last year. In truth, Americans—aside from those who drink in bars, hold girls, and kiss[20] them—do a few good deeds.

25

Shells Toward Chinmen

Skipping rope this week I was able to jump more than two hundred times in one turn. Our class leader, however, can skip more than one thousand times.

From Hsiamen in Fukien Province, the Communists fired fifteen shells towards Kinmen.[21] During lunch, I overheard several teachers discussing this.

The second-grade teacher of A-class said she was very worried that the Taiwan Strait situation could lead to war. But the sixth-grade teacher of B-class said he didn't think it would happen because Taiwan now has the American Armed Forces to protect it.

The newspaper reported that an American landing vessel has arrived at Kaohsiung.[22] On board is a naval group of the U.S. Marine Corps. The Marines will go to Hengch'un[23] for large-scale war games with our Armed Forces.

I also read that because of the drought, fires are breaking out everywhere in the mountain regions, including in the counties of Hualien, Nantou, Taichung, and Miaoli. The mountain forest zones all have big fires. Today again there were village fields burning in the mountains. Planes dropped two hundred fire-suppressant bombs; and two hundred people helped in the emergency.

26

Japanese Actresses

The Japanese Movie Association is sponsoring a Japanese film festival at the Taipei Great World Movie Theater. In order to protect the seven Japanese movie actresses who will make an on-stage appearance, barbed-wire barricades were set up and military police ordered to the streets around the movie house. At the opening ceremony, the Japanese ambassador gave a speech, and then each country's national anthem played, with scenes from that country on the screen. The newspaper reported that thousands of people wrote to the Japanese Embassy for tickets. The report claimed that if they used Chinese in their letters, they got no response; but if they used Japanese, they received tickets.

My aunt[24], who lives in the movie district, Hsimenting, obtained more than twenty tickets from the Ministry of Foreign Affairs. She wanted us to go see the Sunday matinee *Farewell the South Country* and, in the evening, *The Meiji Emperor and General Toyotomi Hideyoshi*.

Mother says Japanese are outstanding people. They recently produced the fastest electronic calculator in the world. However, I don't like Japanese people. The Japanese killed thousands of Chinese.

I'm a patriot.

27

Arbor Day

Today is Arbor Day and the school principal personally planted a tree. Each class was led by a teacher-advisor who planted one tree for the respective class. Even the kindergarten students were represented by a tree.

Mother and Father made a date to meet at the bus station as they wanted to go to our Taipei aunt's home and see tomorrow's

Japanese film festival. In the afternoon after school, Mother saw me off on the Harbor Bureau student bus. I went to her class leader's home, Hu Ling-yu, for a holiday. As the bus started, I regretted leaving Mother. I really miss her.

28

Hide-and-Seek

Hu Ling-yu's mother told me Hu Ling-yu likes me very much, and thinks of me as a younger brother. Hu Ling-yu herself had told this to my mother. My mother also likes her very much. Hu Ling-yu and I have spoken several times. I like her and I would like to be a younger brother to her. However, I didn't say this.

Yesterday evening I didn't sleep well. The reason is that the family played mahjong all night. Whenever I would just about fall asleep, the noise of shuffling mahjong tiles would come from downstairs and disturb me. It sounded like a hard rain. At daybreak it was raining for real.

Hu Ling-yu told me that she was originally planning to take me today to the Harbor Bureau Military Dependents' Village to visit some of our classmates. But because of the rain, she found several students who wanted to come over and play hide-and-seek. A number of times, Hu Ling-yu took me with her to the clothes cabinet to hide. I could smell some kind of strong sweet scent on her body.

29

An Unhappy Situation

At the latest weekly meeting, the principal asked the fifth-grade teacher of A-class, Mr. Liu, to give a talk. He spoke on group social life. He told us that people are born into a particular social environment and cannot have a livelihood without others. The greatest part of our behavior derives from biology and society—these two determining factors. Biology has to do with our senses, the whole nervous system and glands. These are easiest to examine. Society's influences are harder to see, but our behavior is nonetheless influenced in many ways by society. For example, our way of doing certain things, our pursuit of certain goals, or the viewpoints we hold about other people—all these are shaped by the social environment.

I forget much of it. After school, on the way home, I asked Mother about Teacher Liu's talk. She said she thinks he means that every person's thoughts and behavior are unconsciously influenced by the environment, including by the expectations of every kind of organization. And this influence creates a kind of fixed character or personality. If an individual and a group, for example, share the same judgments, attitudes, and expectations, then society is safer and more secure.

But there are some persons, Mother said, who have special creative talent, and if there is only this group organization or institutional life, it can be dangerous for such persons. "I'm saying this is an unhappy situation," she said, "but just for the moment you can't understand."

"How is it unhappy?" I asked.

"Don't worry," Mother said, patting my head. "I will watch out for you."

30

Seed the Clouds

Rain again today. These two days of fresh rains have relieved the long drought in the North and dampened the parched fields of the farmers. Drought conditions are gradually—but definitely— easing. However, in Central Taiwan, the weather is still clear. The most seriously hit areas are the counties of Changhwa, Taichung, and Nantou in central Taiwan. Lots of farms there have not yet been plowed and sowed. With regard to Taiwan's granaries, if no plowing and sowing takes place in Changhwa, Premier Chen Cheng says we will have a serious crisis on our hands. In the South, farms have been ninety-four percent plowed and sowed, but the supply of irrigation water is insufficient. Besides using groundwater, the provincial government wants to seed the clouds for rain.

31

Ration Cards

Because of the drought, the prices of foodstuffs have gone up. The government has put large quantities of foodstuffs on the market, and at each key township it will handle rationing. Township district offices will give every household one ration card for buying rice. Every household—with a proof-of-head-of-household seal—can make purchases at retail stores within the district. According to the regulations, one household with no more than three persons can buy five kilograms worth with one ration card. Households with four to six persons can buy ten kilograms; seven to nine persons, fifteen kilograms; ten persons and above, twenty kilograms.

32

We Can Gamble One More Round

The class leader at noon changed into new clothes. The clothing was small and didn't fit him. He looked very handsome, however. We boys all felt he was handsome and everyone praised his clothes. The class leader was very happy. Who could have known that several girls from Harbor Bureau and First Villages—including pretty Chen Shau-wei—would tease him in front of everyone and would say to his face, "That's girls' clothing," and laugh.

After they said this, the rest of us suddenly understood and began laughing, too. The student leader then became very unhappy.

I believe none of us had any spiteful intent, except Chen Shau-wei. She competes with the class leader in every class for first and second ranking, and she never wins. No matter what we may think, though, I truly can't understand the reason our student leader was wearing girls' clothes.

"I think the clothing is his younger sister's," Mother later said. "Did you also laugh at him?"

"I don't know. I guess I laughed along with everyone else."

"Li-li," Mother said, "I hope you understand that the children of these poor families always have a very difficult time maintaining their self-respect."

The grocery store was located at a point where five roads converged. Under big banyan trees, brick buildings of the village crowded both sides of the main asphalt road. In addition to the grocery, there was a rice-husking building, a farm-tool repair shop, and family farmhouses. Beyond this red-brick settlement, the endless Plain of Lanyang[25] stretched out like a gold-colored sea.

When the proprietor of the grocery store gave Li-li a packet of brown crystal sugar, he asked, "Haven't I seen you before? Where do you come from?"

"Chinshih Village."

"Oh. And who is your grandfather?"

"Yang T'ien-k'uei."

"You must be the son of Pau-ch'i. Your face resembles hers."

The proprietor's wife then asked, "Is your mother Pau-ch'i? Yang Pau-ch'i?"

Li-li nodded.

"Oh, so that's it. You really do look like your mother. She and I sat across from each other in public school. Did your mother also come back to Ilan?"

Li-li shook his head and said, "I...I came by train on my own."

Leaving the grocery store, Li-li followed the asphalt road a while and then turned off into the fields, taking one of the raised paths[26] that serve as boundaries between paddy plots. A stream flowed beside it. He figured that the stream must go to their village. The water made a sighing and sucking sound. Farther along, on the stream bank, a grove of bamboo whipped in the wind. Surrounding him were undulating waves of rice.

He wondered, "Is this what they call a bumper harvest?" With a sigh of appreciation, he thought, "Everywhere there's so much golden light."

"Let me pass, let me pass," a brusque, hoarse voice snapped behind him. The voice belonged to a withered old man in a big hurry. He wore a broad-brimmed farmer's rain hat with two or three strips of bamboo missing, a yellowed white shirt, and faded black shorts. He carried two woven rectangular baskets of dried fruit, snacks, and fresh fruit—one basket suspended from each end of a flat pole that balanced on his shoulder. The baskets wobbled even when he stood still.

"This is a very strange man," Li-li thought. Watching the peddler's backside, he saw that his calves had protruding veins, and that he wore no socks. Also, his toes stuck out of cloth shoes. Suddenly, Li-li cried out, "Are you going to Chinshih Village?"

The man turned partly around, wrinkling his sad brow, and said, "You said something? What village? Chinshih Village? Later I will, I will, I will. I'll get there, later." And with that, he rushed over a bamboo bridge that spanned the stream, and he disappeared into the rice plants.

From whichever direction the throbbing racket of the threshing machine came, the birds, stuffed with rice, were chased out of the rice paddies to high-tension lines strung from the tall transmission towers that straddled the fields. From there they sang the abundance of the season.

Finished with walking the path between paddies, Li-li finally had reached the outskirts of the village. At a great distance away he saw his grandmother[27] standing in the courtyard of the old farmhouse, holding a parasol, and shielding her eyes with her hand to look about.

"Ah," said Li-li, making an energetic leap upward. His head barely cleared the tops of the rice plants. He hollered, "Over here, Grandma, over here!"

"I thought you might not be able to find the road," his grandmother said, taking his hand with the candy in it and drawing him into the shade of the umbrella.

"Just now I saw a strange man in the fields."

"What strange man?"

"An old scrawny man carrying dried fruit on a pole. Is he the

35

sweetmeats peddler?"

"Looks like a monkey?" asked Grandmother, smiling. "People call him the monkey man because he was born with such ugly looks. Here, Grandma wants to give you this dollar. In a while he will come around to our rice-drying courtyard."

"Little Uncle?"[28]

"He's in the fields, otherwise I would have him ride you on his bike to buy some candy. That would be faster than walking and would get you out of the sun sooner. Right now, though, everybody's working in the fields so he doesn't have the time. In a few days, your Little Uncle can take you around to have some fun. But you must wait two or three days, so go find your Third Uncle. He has some good stories for you. Quick now! He's just come back. He's in the study reading or doing calligraphy."

Third Uncle's study smelled of ink. He was at the desk by the window, practicing calligraphy from a copybook. He had been away at college already two years, but the walls of his study were still adorned with images of persons that he admired, pictures he had cut out of books and magazines.

"Ah, my dear little nephew,"[29] said Third Uncle beaming. "I heard you took the train here by yourself, is that right?"

"I...yes," Li-li said. "I'm already in the fifth grade."

"Time goes fast," Third Uncle said looking down again to write a character. "How did you rank in your class this year?"

"I was second."

"Not bad, but a little different than first." Putting down his brush, Third Uncle extracted several small bank notes from his pocket, "I award you five dollars.[30] Next time for first place you'll get ten. Wait a little while and you can buy something from the peddler; you can buy some candy."

"I saw that pitiful man."

"What pitiful man do you know?" Third Uncle asked, grinning.

"I...I know many persons," Li-li said, pointing to the portraits on one wall. "I know this one, this, this and this," Li-li said.

"They're all musicians."

"This one is what?"

"He's an economist, sociologist, and philosopher."

"What's an economist-sociologist-philosopher?"

"If I told you, you wouldn't understand."

"Oh," said Li-li, turning his head to look out the window.

Outside in the fenced yard for raising pullets, two or three groups of chickens were hiding under the guava trees. Bunched together in the shade of the trees, the chickens opened their beaks and puffed their cheeks in and out, breathing and panting. Clusters of ripe emerald fruit glistened on the guava trees. On the other side of the fence between two neatly stacked piles of rice straw, a curly-haired dog was lying flat and dozing. Beyond the bamboo, through a thin opening in the trees, rice fields fluttered and rose with tremendous brightness. The persons working silently in the paddy were largely hidden. Occasionally, from out of the noise of the threshing machine, Li-li could hear snatches of laughing conversation.

"Little Uncle is in the fields?"

"Uh-huh."

"Why don't you work in the fields?"

"I'm a scholar," Third Uncle said. "You and I are both scholars. Remember, we're descendants of those who passed the Civil Service Examination."

"I'd really like to go play in the fields."

"Of course, but the work part is only fun for a little while. It's the kind of work, in fact, that exhausts a fellow. You get muscle pain around the waist and your back aches. Really, it's not so much fun."

Amused, Third Uncle could not suppress a smile. "The weather is very hot. No matter what game you play, you ought to be careful of heat stroke while out in the fields."

Suddenly in the rice fields the noise of the threshing machine approached. A large group of small startled birds flashed into the air and flew away. In the sunny, blue, and cloudless sky, only a vague mist appeared at the edges. Then Li-li saw the marine-blue train, creeping silently across the horizon and, obscured in the mist, the dark green bamboo groves and red brick and tile of two villages—one just beyond the other. Without warning, as though he had leaped out of the landscape, the old peddler appeared, coming fast toward the village on a raised path between fields.

"There's that peddler."

"I didn't hear his voice."

"I just saw him," Li-li said. "He just came out of the fields."

"Indeed, he has arrived," Third Uncle said. "I want to eat a little flavored ice. Come on, we'll go get an ice."

The peddler went into the corner of the big rice-drying courtyard, put down his load beneath a tall wax-apple tree,[31] wiped the sweat from his face with a bandanna, and began calling people, using a revolving bamboo-tube noisemaker fitted with a rubber band and striking board.

The sun was high over the courtyard of the farmhouse. Beyond the shade of the trees, the concrete of the courtyard radiated heat, and the newly cut rice, scattered and spread there, glared blindingly.

Lots of children, with thoughts of flavored candies and ices, scampered out from their homes. A number of fun-seeking young people also hurried out of the nearby fields. The peddler quickly emptied his ice bucket and sold some candy, dry fruit, and two pineapples. He rested for a spell and then started a gambling game for money with the high-spirited youths. The object of the game was to match thin iron strips painted yellow, red, blue, or white on their ends.

Li-li and Third Uncle sat on a platform which held a stone commemorative tablet, eating their flavored ices. The stone tablet platform was one of a pair at the front corners of the rice-drying courtyard. Originally scholars flew flags on the platform to show they had passed the Civil Service Examination.[32] The flag staff was already rotted away from years of wind, rain, and drought. On the stone tablet, however, a person could still see clearly enough the year in which a scholar had passed the examination and could read the scholar's name.

"What kind of game are they playing?" Li-li asked.

"I don't know," Third Uncle said. "I don't play it."

After several rounds of alternating cheers and groans, the youths had emptied their pockets and had lost their competitive spirit. In an orderly row along a stretch of bamboo fence, they sat joking and talking with each other. The peddler, who continued to work the noisemaker inviting people to come, could not help but smile, his mouth revealing badly discolored snags that passed for teeth.

"He looks quite happy," Li-li noted.

"Yes," Third Uncle said. "He won those fools' money; but he

won't win mine."

"Hey! What's up with these young folks? Did they lose?" In front of the rice-drying courtyard, Li-li's Second Uncle had burst onto the scene on a motorcycle. Dismounting, the young veterinarian said, "This monkey, I know how to fix him."

Those observing this were heartened, but after only three turns of play, the veterinarian became discouraged. "Li-li," he said. "Come here. You gamble with him a few turns."

"I don't want to," Li-li said. "I don't know how."

"Nonsense, you can learn," the vet said. "You've got to learn a little bit about everything."

"I don't like gambling," Li-li said. "We are descendants of scholars."

"I know, I know. Everybody around here's a descendant of scholar Yang. Come on, don't you hear what Second Uncle's saying?"

"All right." Li-li leaped down from the stone tablet. "A simple game and just one turn."

"What's this one-turn business? When I say stop, then you can," the vet said, and then turned to the peddler. "What about several straightforward turns? How about it?"

"All right, as you say," the vendor said, and he smiled again with his mottled, yellow teeth. Then with confidence he said, "One jar, I'll bet one jar. This jar of plums is worth seven dollars."

"Including the jar?"

"The jar?"

"Uh-huh. Naturally including the jar. Otherwise, if we win, what can we carry the plums in?"

"All right, all right, pick one. That'll be nine dollars including the jar," the vendor said, vigorously shaking the bamboo tube with the iron strips. "Begin."

Li-li, with trembling hand, drew out one strip and gave it to the vet. He observed a strange expression on the face of the peddler; then, when the vet raised up the marker to display the color, the peddler's face fell, and the surrounding voices of the youths boomed in the air.

"I'm really very sorry," Li-li said to the peddler.

The vet laughed and said, "Yes, he's in a bad way now."

The peddler, his face red, said, "Win or lose, there's always another battle."

In the following ten rounds, Li-li lost only twice, and the peddler lost all the jars.

Lifting up the basket of dishes and peeking in it, the vet said, "You still have some capital...and three pineapples."

A bead of muddy blue-black sweat rolled down the vendor's dark and rigid face.

"This time, we won't gamble for money," the vet said seriously. "We'll gamble for goods. If we win, the three pineapples return to us; if you win, the jars all return to you."

"The jars and the dried fruit inside?"

"Naturally, naturally."

"With a deep sigh of relief, the vendor said, "Good, we'll gamble three turns, okay?"

"As you say," the vet said smiling. "Li-li, is that okay?"

Li-li, withdrawn and despondent, didn't speak.

"Okay, okay," said Third Uncle, leaping down from the stone tablet, his face red and swelling. "You've already played enough to break even. All the sweetmeats go back to him. Let him go."

"Hey! What are you so anxious about. He still has a chance," the vet said. "Go ahead and start, Li-li. Go ahead."

Li-li wiped the warm sweat from his face. The peddler's hand on the bamboo tube with the markers caused it to make a trembling sound.

"Start the game," said the vet. "Start the game."

The peddler suddenly said, "If we just gamble one turn, that's all right with me. Let one turn decide who wins or loses. My heart can't take three turns."

"All right," the vet said. "All right. Pick a marker."

Taking a quick glimpse at the color of the marker, the peddler gnashed his teeth and winced. Finally, feeling the marker lightly with his fingers, he looked again. Having seen the color, he gripped the marker in the palm of his hand, and struck his chest repeatedly. "Take...take it; it's gone. It's always all gone."

"Forget it, forget it," Third Uncle said, "Give it all back to him."

"You idiot," the vet said. "If you can't follow the customs, don't hang around. What are you complaining about anyway?" He moved his hand and took the three pineapples.

"Wait a bit, wait a bit," Li-li said. "We can gamble one more round, gamble for your baskets. If you lose, your baskets stay with us; win, and all the sweetmeats return to you, and all our winnings return to you. What do you think?"

"It's interesting," said the vet. "It's interesting," and touched Li-li's head, saying, "You learn well. You've become almost a professional, my dear nephew."

"You explain well…. Hurry, say okay, just say okay," Li-li said urgently to the peddler. "You still have a chance."

Because of Li-li's earnestness, the group roared with laughter. The vendor, also smiling, said, "Okay, I don't believe my luck can be so bad. All right, come on. I'll give everyone these sweetmeats in the basket if you win. And you can even take the baskets. I…well…I then naturally go home empty-handed."

"Yes," the vet said, "If you lose, then you can carry the empty ice bucket in one hand, and in your other hand…your head carries the battered hat, and your raised hand supports the shoulder pole. That should look very interesting."

"All right, all right, all right," the vendor said. "Come on, child."

When the outcome was known once again, the youths, laughing loudly, snatched up their spoils and ran off into the fields. The peddler, left behind, shook his head and sighed.

"I chose the wrong one. Where should I go? I've lost face. What's left for me?"

The vet said, "Today, I am assuming…well, today you should just leave us here. Tomorrow, come back and we'll talk this over." Then patting Li-li's shoulder he said with a laugh, "My dear nephew, today was interesting. I reward you with five dollars."

"I don't want it," Li-li said. "I don't want it."

"How strange. All of a sudden you seem angry," the vet said. "This was fun. I'm going home before the hot sun burns my bare head and the glare of the grain blinds me."

He straddled the motorcycle and slowly rode out of the court-yard. The peddler already had walked far into the field, the trunk of his thin body hidden deep in the undulating waves of rice. All that could be seen of him now was the pole moving on his shoulder and the tattered broad-brimmed hat. He resembled a scarecrow.

"You needn't feel sad," Third Uncle said, patting Li-li's head. "There was no way to resolve this thing. His luck was just too bad. He only needed to win once, then everything would have been fine. But his luck was too bad. Isn't that so? Isn't it?"

"Yes," Li-li said, watching the departing peddler. "He only needed to win once and then everything would have been all right."

33

Father's Voice

Starting today, Hu Ling-yu will be staying at our house for one week because her father has taken her mother to America on a business trip.

Next Monday our first monthly examinations begin. Once again we won't be able to return to our house in town. It has already been a long time since I've seen Father or heard his voice. He hasn't called the last two evenings.

34

Noodles and Dumplings

Mother says that in the evenings we must begin reviewing for the examinations. This means, however, that on Saturday afternoon we will still be able to go out and play.

After school Mother, Hu Ling-yu, and I, plus a student from First Village, ate noodles and steamed meat dumplings at the student canteen by the little public park just off the school grounds. Afterward, Mother went to the library, and we went to First Village to play.

First Village houses are laid out in rows, layer upon layer along a road that climbs a mountain. The courtyard has a short wall and lots of trees and shade. At the doorway of the home of the chief engineer's, we played old-hawk-grabs-young-chicken.[33]

35

The Highest Grade

In the morning, Hu Ling-yu and I quizzed each other on the subjects to be tested. Occasionally I made a small mistake, but Hu Ling-yu answered correctly every time. I asked her why she did her lessons so perfectly, and she said that every time she failed to get the highest grade on an exam, her parents scolded her when she came home. I have never been scolded because of my test scores. Father only asks that I keep within the top five. And if I receive a perfect score in math and don't make any mistakes in Chinese, I'm allowed to read outside books and I'm free to play.

36

Exam Paper

Cheng Ch'ing-shan sits next to me across the aisle. During the math test, he peeked at my test paper. He's very near-sighted, yet he still doesn't wear glasses. Numerous times he leaned over me, squinting, and almost stuck his face in my exam paper.

Today in two subjects I had perfect scores.

Before going to sleep I want to read another section of *Treasure Island*. I especially love this story of pirates.

37

Some Mothers

In the Chinese test today I didn't get a perfect score. I omitted one word. I don't know how I messed up. I must have been writing too fast. What a pity. How strange.

Hu Ling-yu had perfect scores in all her subjects.

In the evening we were talking in the yard. Hu Ling-yu asked

Mother why she doesn't have another child, a girl. Mother says she really wanted one, but one never came. Once before, I asked Mother why Hu Ling-yu's family didn't have a son. Mother said Mrs. Hu wasn't able to have children. Hu Ling-yu is adopted.

It's really strange how some mothers can have many children; others can have only one; and some mothers none at all!

Hu Ling-yu says she especially likes the peaceful evenings at our house. It's not like hers where someone is always playing mahjong, and there's so much noise.

She said that when it rains at her house the trees in the forest on the mountainside make a loud rattling sound. Several days before, at the village of Kung Liao, a rainstorm suddenly started a flood. A great mountain torrent washed away, or ruined, more than thirty *chia*[34] of paddy fields, as well as four bridges. Two houses were also mostly destroyed. The newspaper said that Taiwan, in the last several years, either doesn't get rain and has a drought, or gets rain and has a flood.

One specialist says this is the result of years of over cutting forests, of illegal felling of trees, and of fires. I asked Mother what's the connection between forests and droughts and floods. Mother said the roots of trees and grass absorb water. They have the effect of regulating and protecting water and soils.

38

Night Snack

The National Assembly[35] elected President Chiang to a third term. The voting was carried out enthusiastically. Some Assembly representatives who are ill—despite having to sit in wheelchairs, or even to be carried on stretchers from hospitals to the Assembly Hall—came to cast their votes and see our President Chiang.

After school Mother took Hu Ling-yu and me to town to see *The Circus of Flying Heaven*. Before the movie began, the theater showed a newsreel of the National Assembly's election of the president.

When the movie was over, we went to Miao K'o[36] for a night snack. Unexpectedly, near the doorway of a seafood restaurant, we ran into Father and several foreigners. There were also several strange-looking women with them. Father said good-bye to his friends immediately, and we returned home together.

Father probably had drunk too much and his mind wasn't clear. In the street on the way home, he muttered that he didn't like the kind of presidential election just held. Hearing this made Mother nervous. She urged him not to talk loosely on the street, and to hurry home, take a bath, and go to bed. However, once home, Hu Ling-yu played our piano and Father sobered up.

For half the night, the two of them played the piano and sang.

39

How Does Someone Become a Captain?

After school, we took a pedicab to the train station to meet Father. He invited us to eat Japanese food. He especially likes Hu Ling-yu. Last night several times he kiddingly said he wanted her to be his goddaughter.

During the meal, he and Mother spoke to each other in Japanese. Finally, very formally, he quietly asked Hu Ling-yu something.

"Good!" said Hu Ling-yu. Then she added very happily, "Li-li then becomes my younger brother. When my mother returns, I will talk with her about this at once. She certainly will want to have Li-li and me change places."

Father and Mother again spoke to each other in Japanese. Finally, they dropped the subject. I felt Father couldn't really like the idea of exchanging me. I also didn't like the notion of becoming the godson of mahjong players.

After dinner, we sat in the seaside park in front of the train station to enjoy the harbor night scene. I quietly spoke with Mother about my feelings. Mother hugged me, saying not to worry. She said Father was only joking.

In the inner harbor several small boats were anchored, including a customs revenue boat, a communications boat, and tugs. These boats appeared very tired, as if they were being rocked in a cradle and had slept the whole day. On the other side of the harbor were merchant ships and warships. These large ships were docked close behind one another at a wharf. Ship lights were reflected upside down and waving on the water's surface. The glow of the ships' lights framed in gold the night view of the sea.

Father smoked a cigarette and appeared to have no interest in talking. I don't know why, but every time watching the sea at night, he seems unhappy. We only sat there for a while, then went to the last evening showing of a movie called *A Hero in a Time of Anarchy and Disorder*. The movie was about the era of a Russian Czar. The film was great, with scenes of cavalry fighting on a huge plain and a ship burning on a river. It was very inspiring.

Boys should want to be heroes.

They were a group of four persons: a captain, a chief mate in the lead, and Li-li and his uncle[37]—a younger brother of Li-li's father—following behind. They went up a narrow flight of stairs and entered a dark bar.

"Welcome, welcome!" said the waiter, awakening from an afternoon nap. Hurried and flustered, he sang out, "May I ask how many persons?"

"Three adults," said the captain. Then, patting Li-li's shoulders, he added, "and one boy scout."

Everyone in the room laughed.

The waiter guided them through an arrangement of several sofa-like chairs to a table by a window. The interior of the room was filled with the smell of years of thick cigarette smoke, stale alcohol, and spoiled meat.

"What's the strange smell?" the captain asked. Then in a loud roar, "Hey. Where's all the girls?"

"The girls will be here soon," the waiter said. Bowing at the waist with hands folded in front of him. "Just open the window and turn on the fan, and you won't notice the smell."

"But I don't understand. How can you have this putrid smell in

here?" complained the chief mate.

"It must be the smell of zombies," said the captain, and several persons laughed. "What do we want to drink?"

"Really, I can't drink anything. It's crazy," the chief mate said, "I'm still amazed we three and half persons just ate two hundred dumplings."[38]

"I think we can eat even more," said the captain, rolling up the long sleeves of his white shirt and taking out a handkerchief. His forehead and cheeks were perspiring, and there was sweat on the front and back of his neck. "Well, are we going to eat another hundred dumplings or what?"

"Please," Li-li's uncle said. "Forget the dumplings. We've had enough."

"Ah, yes. Another hundred dumplings and we'll all become like Chu Pa-chieh,[39] the famous pig," the captain said. "Let's drink whiskey on the rocks."

Li-li gazed out the opened window at two eagles circling in the air over the harbor. The afternoon sunlight shone brightly in the early summer sky and on the harbor and its painted ships. Through a wide gap in the surrounding hills, Li-li could see farther out into the harbor. The sea breeze brushed his face lightly and refreshingly. In a happy, expansive mood, he felt the joy of imagining all his ambitions fulfilled.

"How does someone become a captain?" Li-li asked.

"You should be able to eat one hundred dumplings and drink, let's say, two bottles of whiskey," the captain answered with a smile. Then he added, "Not really, not really. I can't joke with our little friend. Bravery and daring, Chief Mate. Isn't that it? One must be brave."

"I don't know," the chief mate said. "When I'm on duty, I'm mostly just bored. I don't want to be a captain. In fact, the next time ashore, I'm going to quit and wash my hands of this whole dirty business."

"I've already heard you say that several times," the captain said. "Yet every time…well, you get to thinking of those girls on the docks. You don't want to `do' the sea, but you still want to `do' the girls."

"We can lead the youngster astray," Li-li's uncle inserted. "Gentlemen."

47

"I don't want to `do' girls," Li-li said. "But I want to `do' the sea."

"Child, why do you want to `do' the sea?" asked the captain.

"I want to travel around the world."

"Yes, it's true we have seen many places," the captain said. "Isn't that so, Brother Ching-sheng?" directed at Li-li's uncle.

"We have had some happy days," Li-li's uncle responded. "Very happy days." The expression on his face, however, did not mirror this. Then, as the captain and the chief mate began a drinking game, he touched Li-li's head lightly and said, "If you want to be a captain you should know the stars. And you must be brave."

"I know," Li-li said. "Although one of your boats sank, you are brave. But if you had piloted a wooden boat then it wouldn't have sunk."

Choking back a laugh, the captain blew out a mouthful of whiskey, then said, "I once sank a wooden boat, so I changed to sailing a steel one. No matter what kind of boat, though, they really all can sink. Little Friend, you can damage them by bumping into something, turning them over, or burning them down."

"Uncle, how did your boat sink?"

"It burned," Li-li's uncle said. "It burned and broke apart."

"To tell you the truth, I really envy you, Ching-sheng," said the captain. He went on thoughtfully, "During my life on the sea, I have seen the most beautiful and impressive sights. Like lotus flowers floating on the surface of the sea; or three boats floating in the vicinity of a great sea bloom; or when six or seven boats were on the horizon at one time; or even better, the time when I saw several ships slowly appearing at the same time from beyond the horizon. I consider it lucky to see even one other ship far out at sea."

"Right. And to be a captain you should also know how to swim," the chief mate said.

"And be able to swim a very long way. Isn't that so, Ching-sheng?"

"I think it's necessary, yes," Li-li's uncle said.

"But if you're lucky, then you won't need to swim very far," Li-li said.

"Right, luck can also determine whether you get a good `old lady,'" the captain said. "Ching-sheng's luck is good; he has a fine `old lady.'"

"My luck also isn't so bad," put in the chief mate. "I have an 'old lady' in every port."

"Numbers do not make up for quality?" the captain said. "Do you understand what we are talking about, Little Friend?"

"You are talking about girls."

"Yes, yes. Your comment about luck reminded me," the captain said. Then in a loud voice to the waiter, "Hey, young man, what about the girls?"

"Very soon," the waiter said. "I'll get them on the telephone immediately. How many do you want?"

"Three adults and one child," the captain said.

40

Like a Prophet

This noon, while eating lunch at the school canteen, I heard several male teachers debating preparations to privatize four big state-owned textile factories. These teachers often discuss topics like this during lunch. Thanks to my reading the newspaper every day, I'm able to understand a lot of what they say.

Most of the young teachers live in a bachelors' dormitory fronting the near road. Originally built for factory workers, it still houses many single employees. The canteen is open to all of them, but it's the teachers and students who most regularly go there to eat. These days, Mother cooks dinner only occasionally. We eat most of our meals at the canteen. Naturally, on the weekend, Mother does all the cooking. She prepares very special dishes then, which she says are highly nutritious and can balance my weekly diet.

The teachers always sit together, and they know me. Sometimes one of them will misquote something from the newspaper and I will correct him. Of course, they talk of things I can't fully understand. For example, one teacher said that with nationalized enterprises, the welfare of workers is better. His company, for instance, has an alternative public school, employees' dormitory, health clinic, canteen, library, and an auditorium which soon will show movies every evening.

Another teacher said that the whole country, however, has many persons who are seeking a means of support or subsistence. Privatization can raise worker productivity, increase profits, enrich society, and create more movie theaters, schools, and libraries.

These things I don't really understand.

A while ago, there was a teacher who was very intense. Every time he said something, the others just sat in silence and listened. He was at our school for only two weeks, then went abroad to study. I remember he was sort of like a prophet and would confidently declare, for instance, that with the advancements in the textile industry, we have already seen female laborers from the villages swarm to the factories. As a result, light industry of every kind has increased its speed of development, including electronics, electric machinery, cement, and foodstuffs. In the future, even more village laborers—but this time males—will be similarly drawn. He said: "The collapse of agricultural society is coming."

Today there is a piece of news that probably has some connection to what he said. The newspaper says that America has developed a loan program with an appropriation of ten million U.S. dollars. To spur our country's privatization of enterprises, America will lend funds for the establishment of new factories and for new equipment. Export-processing enterprises can obtain preferential loans.

41

Big Hugs

Hu Ling-yu today did not come home with us. Her father returned from abroad this morning. At noon after classes, a special chauffeur-driven car took her home. Her mother gave me half a dozen American apples and some new clothes, but I felt a little lonely. When Hu Ling-yu feels happy she likes to give me big hugs. The feeling is very nice. I hope this weekend will pass quickly. On Monday I can see her again.

In the afternoon, Mother went to the library. The principal

has invited her to give a talk at the next weekly assembly. She went to the library to find information for her speech. So, I stayed after school to play. There are always some students around to play with.

Recently it has rained hard without let-up, so we haven't been able to play outdoors. Inside the school, kids in the highest grade began playing war horse in the hallways. This game is very simple. The tallest and biggest student carries a classmate on his back. The classmate should be small, athletic, and clever. He must battle with another horse and rider, and push the rider off. The team whose rider falls off first loses. Some teams fight and knock each other down. Others battle more than one horse and rider at the same time, which often leads to wide-scale war involving many teams.

The twenty minutes between classes is devoted to this game. During the hour-long rest period at noon, time is also devoted to war horse. These battles are fought all over the school right up to the last possible minute before we're called back to class.

In our class the fiercest team is Chang Ta-lung, as the war horse, ridden by the class leader. Ta-lung[40] is a big kid and the class leader is very small. Their team is especially difficult to defeat. The student leader grasps the waist of Ta-lung tightly with his feet, while Ta-lung's strong arms lock tightly the knees of the class leader. They have also developed clever moves.

The school has two ball fields, single and double horizontal bars, and a long-jump sand pit, but there isn't any running track. Because the mountain slope is covered with trees and shrubs and knee-high grass, it's perfect for games of hide-and-seek and tag.

This afternoon not so many students stayed after school to play. A few were in an empty classroom playing card games and marbles. Some others took turns going to the dormitory of the sixth-grade teacher of A-class to get help with their lessons. A couple students were in the music room studying piano with their teacher. With no one in particular to play with, I went to a classroom and sat down and read *Treasure Island*.

Because I had no noon nap, I went straight to bed after supper without taking a bath, and I slept half the night. I was awakened by the noise of Father coming home. He had brought three friends and two hunting dogs with him. Several days earlier, returning to our house in town, Father and I were talking when we saw the father of my classmate Cheng Ch'ing-shan. He had caught a deer using a trap. Father said he himself would like to hike up the backside of our mountain and take a look around.

42

Are You Brave Enough to Do This by Yourself?

Father wants to take me up the mountain, but I have already arranged to go today to our class leader's home to play.

The class leader's home is very small. Third Village has more than ten rows of housing projects, each unit very small. The rows of unlandscaped housing sit alone on muddy ground. About five hundred workers and their families live there. A few trees can be seen on the opposite riverbank, but on the side of the projects all the trees must have been cut when the houses were built.

One time after school, the class leader and I and several classmates took advantage of the factory guard's not being at his post, and we sneaked through the big gate. The factory occupies a very large area. To cut through its grounds on the way home is faster than to go around on the road. There are offices in the front section of the factory for the high-level managers who live in First Village. Here also are some lower-level employees who live in Second Village. The factory workers live in Second Village and Third Village.

The student leader's father works in the metal-casting section. When we went to see him, that section was stifling hot. There's a blast furnace in the front, and the workers use a suspended cart, or ladle, to pour pig iron into the sand of the cast-iron dies. Every classmate who passes through the factory grounds tries to find his own father. Some are in the oxygen section, some are in the coal section, and some are in the carbide section. So many sections.

The student leader's family includes four brothers and one younger sister. I looked around their house and it certainly seemed crowded. A sign is nailed to the front door that says: District Representative of the Community Unit. The student leader's father also knows how to do massage and set broken bones and the like. On Sundays their house overflows with people, including his brother's junior high classmates, who come to study. I don't like these junior high students. They remind me of troublemakers or juvenile delinquents.

When I went to see the class leader, he was reading a pile of comic books about swordsmen. His second brother, with several friends, was also crowded on the wooden bed reading the comics. In addition, some classmates were playing marbles in the mud. They had scooped out three small depressions in the earth and said they were playing "Tiger Enters the Cave."

Suddenly at noon, air-raid sirens went off to mark the beginning of a defense drill. The class leader's family had just begun eating lunch. I saw a dish of green vegetables on the lunch table. There was also one dish with nothing but pieces of stewed beef and potatoes, as well as one dish that I didn't know. His mother invited me to join them, but I politely refused. I had to go home and eat with Mother.

Father returned home a little later in the afternoon. He said the noon air-raid drill had brought him and a friend some good luck. When the sirens began, it spooked a group of mountain deer from the brush. The deer bolted right into view. Altogether, Father and his friend killed two of them, including one with big antlers. They also killed three fat foxes.

Amid the sound of light jingling bells, the train slowly pulled away from the small platform. It emerged from the station at a point where one end of a small market bordered the tracks.

"At about thirty meters," Li-li's father said, "your gun will miss to the right of the target by two centimeters. About thirty meters, or from here to that grocery store. Can you see the store?"

"I can see it," Li-li said. "When I aim at a target, I should aim two centimeters to the left. Is that right?"

"You also must hold the gun tightly against the hollow of your shoulder," the doctor warned. "Otherwise you won't hit the bird in the tree, and you may," he said with a laugh, "hit the wild boar on the ground."

They stepped down from the train station platform, crossed over to the far tracks, and began walking down the ties. They soon entered the market, which stretched irregularly down a road with buildings on both sides.

In the town's narrow streets, students were heading to class, adults to work, and vendors and peddlers to market. Two floppy-eared hunting dogs led the hunting party. Sometimes the dogs bumped and jostled one another; other times they were preoccupied with investigating scents along the road and in the nooks and crannies of the brick walls. With their large mouths and tongues, they often startled people on the street. The doctor continually shouted commands, hurrying them along, not wanting them to linger. On his large head, the plump doctor wore a brimless hunting cap that left the back and front of his neck exposed. From beneath the cap, the gray roots of his hair were exposed. The hunting gun, which he carried slung over his plump shoulder, flashed whenever it caught the light. Li-li's father carried two guns, one on each shoulder, and a full ammunition belt around his waist. Both men wore short pants, thick white long-sleeved shirts, and high boots.

"I'm pretty much tired of hunting wild boars," the doctor said. "Some day we ought to get some other men and go into the mountains in the eastern section to hunt something else. I tell you, that damn unnerving roar of a wild boar can make even the mountains tremble. Do you think you're brave enough to go hunting, Li-li?"

Li-li scratched his forehead. His face reddened.

"Scared?" laughed the doctor. "It's all right. As soon as one speaks about it, one becomes frightened."

They came out of a narrow alley near the marketplace. The two hunting dogs bounded toward the glistening light of a pond. From the bank, they lapped up water and soon began to paw at the fish and shrimp in the pond or to catch sight of their own reflections and bark.

On a small road, the group worked their way around the pond's long spears of mixed grasses to the foot of a mountain. They headed toward a high valley. In the lengthening forest shadows, cicadas and bird cries could be heard all around them. The surface of the mountain road was filled with small, irregular patches of sunlight wherever the shadows of trees did not fall and cover it.

"Can I try my gun out, Dad?"

"I'll try it first," said the doctor, taking the bird gun from Li-li's father. "I should aim two centimeters to the left of the target, right?"

"Uh-huh, at a distance of about thirty meters," the father said.

With one shot, the doctor destroyed all trace of the red cicada, which, in its beautiful new color, had been clinging to the black trunk of a tree. "This gun isn't bad," said the doctor. "Li-li, you try and hit that green one."

Li-li took aim at the cicada on the tree trunk. He shot twice. The bluish-green cicada was still there, still drumming with its abdomen, singing. Li-li's father took the gun and with one shot obliterated it. The bright background of the sky sharply defined the edges of the tree trunk.

"I can't hold my gun steady," Li-li said, his face reddening from shame.

"The gun's very heavy," the doctor said. "You should eat lots more rice and grow big faster." From his shoulder, he took his own hunting rifle. "I'll try this gun."

The gun roared. A perching island thrush[41] was knocked out of a tree. Simultaneously, the whole forest awoke with a mad beating of wings and bird cries. From the shade of the trees flew out a white-backed woodpecker, a tawny wren warbler, a rufus-breasted blue flycatcher, a rusty-cheeked scimitar babbler, a gray-throated minivet, a Muller's barbet, a blue magpie, and a Japanese green pigeon. The entire sky filled with frantic, whirling resplendence. At the same time, the hunting dogs barked uncontrollably in pursuit of other game and soon flushed several fat bamboo chickens from the grass and underbrush.

"Shoot, Li-li," the doctor shouted, as he himself fired into the mass of flying birds.

Li-li's shot only snapped off part of a branch. The gunfire echoed through the trees and along the road. Then the forest was silent. A terrified magpie was still flying, but without a sound, and suddenly even the small vivid patches of sunlight in the green shade vanished.

They continued on into the deepest part of the mountain valley. The farther they went in the forest, the more secluded it became. Along the road, the two hunting dogs picked up another scent in the grass and underbrush and began sobbing low. After a moment, they found a tree trunk with rub lines and gouges. Sniffing the air, they howled and leaped into the underbrush.

"I can also smell that scent," the doctor said, taking up his rifle. He sniffed the air with zest. "Can you smell it, Li-li?"

"I only smell the rotten leaves on the ground."

"Yes, yes, but there's another kind of smell," the doctor said. "I think we'll soon be in a real fight. Are you afraid?"

"I'll be behind both of you."

"You stay right behind your father," the doctor said. "Don't get so nervous that when you shoot your bird rifle, you hit me in my big bottom." He laughed and added, "Or my little bird." He walked ahead, quickening his pace.

The hunting dogs suddenly lapsed into a fit of wild barking. But they soon seemed to have run into trouble, and their feverish barking turned to low, deep whimpering.

The dogs, as they saw the wild boars approaching, maneuvered to form a line of attack. Each boar had a bristling mane and ferocious teeth. The doctor called out to the dogs as he raised his gun and aimed. Because of the close presence of their master, the dogs were emboldened, and they leaped fearlessly toward the boars.

The doctor shot once and knocked down a panicky sow. The bullet hit its left buttock and the beast struck the ground with its throat, then somersaulted. The foul-smelling blood splattered everywhere.

Li-li's father shot a big boar in the forehead. It screamed, then all four legs went limp and it collapsed. In a frenzy, the pack began breaking ranks. Some ran toward recesses of the mountain valley to escape. Others, which had been moving along the outside of the pack as a kind of protective guard, began to turn away from the confrontation as well. But two or three were sufficiently provoked to fight, and they charged and knocked over the dogs, then trampled them.

"Run fast, Li-li!" his father cried, opening fire on a boar coming at them.

Running a short way, Li-li took refuge behind a big tree, then stuck his head out to look. The doctor was wielding the butt of his rifle against one of the boars. Li-li's father had retreated several steps behind the road and was reloading. The hunting dogs, gravely injured, lay on the ground whimpering and struggling to rise. Seeing this, Li-li's

56

father and the doctor momentarily lost their composure.

"Run again! Li-li!" his father shouted, as he fired several more shots into a group of the dark-brown boars. Finally he ran at them, swinging the stock of his rifle.

The doctor retreated to reload. "Goddamn it," he exclaimed. "How did we get into this mess? I've never seen anything like this with boars. This is a real fight."

Li-li again ran a short distance away. This time he stood on the road looking all about him. He saw a boar upend the doctor, striking at his short fat calves. The doctor took another powerful blow to his midsection.

"Damn it to hell," the doctor cried. Then, bringing the gun close to the head of the pig, he fired.

Unconcerned for his own safety, Li-li ran to the doctor, but on seeing the blood flowing into puddles from the doctor's two wounds where the boar's teeth had slashed, he couldn't do anything.

The doctor closed his eyes tightly and clenched his teeth. His face was red and he was sweating profusely.

"Are you all right, Doctor Uncle? Fatty Uncle?"

"I'm..." Forcing his eyes open, the doctor asked, "What about your father?"

At that moment, Li-li's father was being chased by a wild boar. By running evasively, though, he was able to reload again from the ammunition belt.

"He ran in a good direction," the doctor said. "If he had come this way, we would have had a tragedy." He gulped for air a few times, then said, "Take off some clothing and help me bind up my wounds, can you?" Saying this, he loosened his own belt and removed his shirt.

A gun fired a number of times. Then all was quiet in the mountain valley.

Li-li's father appeared. He took a sharp knife from a sheath on his chest and cut away the doctor's underwear. "Li-li, go see about the dogs." Then to the doctor, "How do you feel, Doctor?"

"I feel pretty good," the doctor said, and forced a laugh. "But I need to take a look to be sure."

"The dogs are dead!" Li-li yelled. "They're both dead!"

"All right, come here quick," Li-li's father said.

The doctor used a small bottle of Kaoliang, a sorghum liquor, to wash his left hand and then wash his wounds. Finally, he used his index finger to probe the opening of the wound on the side of his belly.

"It's not too bad," he said. "Fat flesh protects against injury." He laughed and then winced in pain. "I can't even laugh; we better leave here quickly."

"We need to find a couple people to carry you out on a stretcher," Li-li's father said.

"We need a doctor," the doctor replied trying to joke. "You see, a doctor also needs a doctor sometimes."

"You go and find a doctor, Li-li," the father said. "Hurry and run to town and find a doctor. Or just find anyone. Then tell them the situation here in the mountains. Are you brave enough to do this by yourself?"

"I have a gun," Li-li said.

"And you're also a boy."

43

Mother's Lecture

Mother said she wanted to present her speech to the whole school as a part of Children's Day.[42] Because she also hoped that students' parents could read her speech, she bought paper and mimeographed the text. When she gave her talk, copies were passed out to every classmate. Mother was never more formal with me than when we discussed the things touched on in her speech. Now I have some idea how she is educating me.

The key points of her speech:

The upbringing of children and the economic circumstances of their parents do not have the strong connection you might think. Success is determined more by the level of knowledge possessed by the parents and the degree of concern they show their children. We want to encourage our children to be engaged in emotionally meaningful activities and to have close contact and good communication with them. We want to give them our spiritual support. Beyond this, we also must encourage them to have interaction with other children. Children, through play, come to understand how to establish their own methods of learning. At the same time, such play enhances the effectiveness of their study.

An adult's further development in life and the development process of children are similar: both depend on emotionally meaningful activities for a healthy imagination. Both also rely on the examination of the views of others in the gradual process of understanding the defining characteristics of one's self, and in making necessary corrections and improvements.

Her speech, by the way, received very warm applause. Near the end of it, she nearly cried several times. I don't know why.

44

Harbor Steamships

Yesterday after school, Hu Ling-yu came with us again to our house in town. Several days ago, we agreed that she come in the evening and watch the Youth Day. Every time there's a parade, it passes by our house on the big street.

Last night Father did not return. He phoned and said he was in Taipei.

Mother took Hu Ling-yu and me to my paternal grandfather's. Grandpa still looks very grave. He seldom speaks and ordinarily shows no expression on his face. When Mother and I greet him and try to talk to him, he only nods his head. In fact, whenever he meets anyone his reaction is the same.

My uncles, one in high school and the other at college, were in the living room playing a card game. I don't know how to play it. They said it was bridge. Upstairs someone was playing guitar and singing English-language songs.

When Grandmother saw me, she was very happy. She took my hand and asked me about many things. She complained that I hadn't come to visit for a long time. She was also very happy to see

Hu Ling-yu, but because Grandmother only speaks Taiwanese and Hu Ling-yu only speaks Mandarin, they couldn't really talk.

I took Hu Ling-yu to see my former school. It's three times the size of our current school and even the playgrounds are much different. There are four completely equipped baseball diamonds, each occupying one corner of a field. Every weekend and holiday, people in the neighborhood of the school, including adults and middle-school kids, have pick-up games there.

While we were there, several children by the big ditch of water at the edge of the playground were catching loach, a mudfish. Where the water was clear, they would turn over small rocks and usually find them. I also took Hu Ling-yu to see my former classroom in a handsome red-brick building. Our current black-wood classrooms just can't compare. Also unique to my old school are the tall coconut palm trees. They show that the school has a long history.

I don't know why Father doesn't like that school. One thing that's strange, though, is that I can't really remember anything special that happened there, or any special teachers or classmates. But I do remember that the first entry I made in my journal was Father's remark that it was important for a school to have music, art, physical education, and other subjects more in touch with Nature.

Today the newspaper said that 100,000 youths in Taipei's Sun Yat-sen Square[43] celebrated Youth Day. Our Keelung parade was also very exciting. All the schools above middle school joined in. The bands from each school led the way. The girls carried lanterns and the boys held up torches to light the way. Along the route, the marchers sang and chanted slogans continuously. I was very impressed when they sang, "Down with the Russian bandits! Overthrow the Reds!" They also shouted, "Long live the Republic of China. Long live the Three Principles of the People.[44] Long live President Chiang!"

When the tail of the parade had passed our windows, I hoped the ships in the harbor might blow their whistles all at the same time. There was, however, no such rousing salute, only the return of the usual traffic noise. It seems that the steamships in the harbor only sound their whistles like that on Chinese New Year's eve.

45

Communist Spy

Today Cheng Ch'ing-shan didn't come to class. The teacher asked students from his village about this. Finally, one person reluctantly said that Cheng Ch'ing-shan's father had been arrested last night by the police. Our teacher asked why he had been arrested. The student said it was for spying for the Communists. One other person was also arrested.

No classmate dared to go see Cheng Ch'ing-shan. After school Mother and I, on our way home, stopped at his village to see him. When we did this, the Cheng's neighbors regarded us suspiciously. They hid behind the walls around their houses and stole glances at us.

Cheng Ch'ing-shan was inside fanning coal-smoke that was pouring from the stove. His mother was in the kitchen preparing supper. When she saw us, it was as though we were the closest of relatives. Her eyes filled with tears and her nose ran. As soon as she started to cry, the two young girls with her began to cry loudly as well. The scene stunned Mother.

46

Last Night There Was Something Like a Ghost

Father looks unhappy. He says that not long ago he exported some ready-made clothes, but because the manufacturers and business firms did less work and used poorer materials than originally agreed upon, the quality of the clothing is poor. Hong Kong clients have been writing to complain.

After dinner, he and Mother brought up the case of Cheng Ch'ing-shan's father. Mother asked him if there were any friends who could help.

"How can anyone help someone accused of spying for the Communists?" Father said.

"It's not for spying, only for criticizing the government too much. Someone tipped the police off," Mother said. "The family has three children. It's a terrible situation."

"You better just forget about it. You don't want to stir up trouble," Father said. "Involvement with the Communists, subversion, and Taiwan independence are the three crimes for which there is no defense. Even Lei Chen, the nation's most ardent anti-Communist, was falsely accused last year of sheltering spies. He was given ten years' imprisonment. Someone set him up, but he was still given ten years!" Growing angry, he added, "Anyway, in these times, thought, speech, human rights, creativity, learning, and culture...none of these is free."

"All right, all right," Mother said, watching out the open window. Then she stood up and closed it. "We don't want to talk about this affair again."

Li-li's maternal grandmother had been telling a series of interesting stories, but finally it was she, not Li-li, who fell asleep. The noisy snoring of Li-li's grandfather nearby and the croaking of the field frogs in the night made him restless. The air was also humid and stuffy. Several times Li-li looked out the dark window, unable to stop imagining that the wavering shadows of trees might be evil spirits. Then, trembling and holding his breath a moment, Li-li was certain he saw a black shape at the window screen. Li-li was petrified.

The shadowy image faintly cried, "Ma-oom, ma-oom." At the same time, Li-li heard a motorcycle moving fast on the road from the village. The black image suddenly withdrew from the window. Li-li thought he heard dogs begin barking about the same time. In a little while, he began to relax, and soon he became drowsy and fell asleep.

He rolled over in bed several times and finally opened his eyes. Earlier, his sleep had been disturbed by a flock of small birds flying from the ridge of the roof to the courtyard bamboo. From the window he watched them swoop up and down, then hop and dance in the branches and leaves. The bright sky also seemed to shine into his clouded heart. He sighed deeply and finally came from behind the curtain of the old bed.

The sun had already risen above the rooftop, and beyond the back-

yard wall it was burning brilliantly. Because of this, the shade within the wall appeared just that much deeper and cooler. Several women around the well were preparing and arranging chickens, ducks, fruit, and vegetables. These reunited sisters, other relatives, and friends talked of old times as they worked. Their conversation was frequently enlivened with laughter. A small circle of men nearby were smoking and discussing affairs of the nation. Every so often one of them, with hardened face, would express his views, gesturing dramatically, causing raised eyebrows and sidelong glances. Such passion went against the grain of the leisurely discussions.

"Here's Li-li," Grandmother announced. "It's my daughter's darling son."

The women all gave their attention to the boy. He stood on the railing of the back gate, keeping his gaze on the brick well. From below the ground, the spring water gushed up through a hollow bamboo tube to just above the water level of the well. Through the blue-green surface ripples, dense patches of algae, growing on the inside walls of the well, were visible.

"At last you are awake. I can give you some chicken soup and rice congee for breakfast," Li-li's grandmother said, washing her hands and standing up. "Today I'll be very busy worshipping at the temple. I won't have much time to look after you."

As Li-li's grandmother spoke, gongs and drums began sounding beyond the village at the site of the religious ceremonies.

"Last night, a...," Li-li began. "Last night there was something like a ghost, Grandma."

"What ghost?" his grandmother said. "Shhhh. You don't want to scare people."

"Your story, you didn't finish it and fell asleep. I...there was a shadowy figure at the window crying, `Ma-oom, ma-oom.' When it finished moaning, it ran away."

"Ma-oom, ma-oom," repeated the grandmother, looking furtively about. "This ghost business, you don't want to mention it again. It can frighten people. If anyone asks, don't say anything. There's no reason to think it was a ghost. You just dreamed it in your sleep. Relax now and eat your breakfast."

Li-li convinced himself that he must have dreamed or imagined it and, feeling somewhat relieved, began to eat his breakfast. On fur-ther thought, however, he felt that his grandmother had reacted a little too nervously. She had darted out past the backyard to where the field path reached the trees. She was now standing there looking in all di-rections.

After breakfast, Li-li ran to the same spot in the field to take a look. But in the huge fields, he could see only a stream flowing through the landscape and, on its banks, dense bamboo groves. In the field was also a raised mound which was the air-raid shelter.

"What are you looking at, Li-li," asked Little Uncle.

This uncle was still a child. He had climbed high into a guava tree to pick the fruit. Several boys and girls, holding bamboo hats to catch the guavas, waited beneath the tree, their necks craned upward.

"Do you want to come down, Little Uncle?" Li-li asked. "I have something I want to tell you."

"Okay, I'll just pick a few more and then come down," Little Uncle responded. "Do you want one?"

"I don't want one," Li-li said, looking out again past the trees to the fields and the gray, obscure mound of the air-raid shelter covered with thick grass.

"What are you looking at?" Little Uncle asked, sliding down the tree.

Li-li led his uncle away from the trees into the field path, then he said, "Last night I saw a ghost."

"What? You're kidding."

"No, honest. There was a black figure outside my window, crying, 'Ma-oom, ma-oom.'"

"Crying what?"

"Ma-oom."

"Crying Mamma?" Little Uncle asked. "And afterward?"

"The dogs barked and it ran away," Li-li said. "Grandma said I only imagined it, but as soon as I told her, she ran out to look at the air-raid shelter. Don't you think it's strange?"

"Do you want me to keep this a secret? We can't just tell any-one," Little Uncle said, looking quickly around.

About noon, several policemen came to the village. The local coun-try folk—both men and women—poured tea and offered cigarettes,

while those who had returned from the city, or who were college stu-
dents, stood around looking angry.

"The Ministry of the Interior's vice minister is a relative of mine,"
a college student said with a hint of provocation.

"Yes, yes, we know this," one policeman said. "We are here only
to carry out a little government business. We just want to take a look
around, that's all, merely take a look around."

"But if we find who we're looking for, we're still going to arrest
him," another policeman said. "The relative of the vice minister can
do what he likes, but sedition is still sedition. Last night someone saw
him at the bus station."

"Perhaps they were mistaken," Li-li's grandfather said indig-
nantly. Then, out of their hearing, he added, "Such despicable yes-
men."

"Everyone does their best, Grandpa," said Li-li's grandmother.
Then she turned to the policemen and smiled, "If he returns, I cer-
tainly will tell him to surrender. These young people are naive; they
don't understand these things."

"Don't understand these things?" the grandfather said. "You have
a weak brain, woman! If they don't understand these things, how can
they pass the college exams?"

"All right, Grandpa, don't get angry," said the son of the county
government secretary. "It's a holiday. Won't you gentlemen celebrate
a bit with us? Please stay and have something to drink."

"No, no. We have to be off," said the policeman in charge. "Sorry
to have disturbed you, sorry."

From the direction of the village, the drums and gongs of the
religious ceremony from Royal Palace Temple continued to reverber-
ate. Soon, the sound of shrill horns lifted the music higher. But even
though the atmosphere of the celebration for the good harvest was
beginning to permeate the mood of the local people, and even though
the noon meal of wine and complementary dishes was now ready to be
served, nothing could extinguish Grandfather's indignation and bit-
terness. On the contrary, the wine supper made him and a number of
other people even more irritated.

"What kind of a world is this anyway? What kind of real jus-
tice is there?" said an employee of a paper-making factory, his face

flushed with anger. "You people who can be logical, listen to me. Before, because we are Chinese, we risked everything to get the Japanese out. Now that the Japanese have left, must we struggle against the Chinese?"

"Taro is taro," said the grandfather. "A sweet potato is a sweet potato. The mainland Chinese are mainlanders; we Taiwanese are Taiwanese."

But at the mention of Japan, several youths—some sober, some drunk—began to sing a Japanese martial song, overpowering the conversation.

"This is a tragedy. This is the kind of tragedy you get from China's defeat in the war," one professor said with emotion. "Am I right?"

"I'm not too clear about your meaning, but it's certainly a breach of etiquette, Professor," Li-li's Third Uncle said. Then, a little pompously, he added, "When a nation suffers defeat in war, it is even more reason that it should create a serious political, social, and educational system that is competitive with other nations. If a nation can't be serious about these things, the consequences are sure to be tragic."

"When you say tragic, you mean sad," a local youth said bitterly. "My situation is tragic. All I did was speak out against privilege, against terror by those in power, and against corruption. The school dismissed me, goddamn it. With such bad luck, I haven't been able to do anything or go anywhere since. I pass my time wandering the fields. My family is overworked like water buffalo. This, my friends, is tragic."

"You still have had some good luck," the professor said. "No one has said you are a Communist. And you still have the accumulated merit of your ancestors."

As they talked back and forth, someone turned again to the subject of the police search.

"If there was anyone at the bus station who saw Ah-ch'ing, then Ah-ch'ing ought to have come back last night," said one of the group. "The person I saw was the wrong man."

"That boy, Ah-ch'ing, doesn't know where to hide."

"He better not come back here," Grandfather said angrily. "A person like him who doesn't study, gets involved in politics for nothing, loves to talk—if he comes back and runs into me, why, he'll get a poke in the mouth and his legs broken. I can do it."

"Li-li," Grandmother said. "Come here, if you're finished eating. You can help me. Go with me to the temple to worship. Do some of you others want to go now?"

A number of women immediately said yes. One great aunt instructed Li-li, "All small children must go to worship. Then, when they grow up, they will become good scholars."

The group carried thank-you baskets full of the prepared chicken, duck, fish, beef, vegetables, fruit, and sweet cakes. With an air of piety, they walked off across the fields of cut rice. Only stubble, chaff, and spilt grain remained where they walked. The high sun shone golden on the open fields. Gleaning birds formed flocks there and flitted about on the ground. At intervals, near the front of the temple, a string of firecrackers suddenly flashed and exploded in the air.

The small temple was located beneath a banyan tree at a crossroads. Being set among the fields, the temple was not often frequented. But now, persons from all corners of the village passed in an endless procession, trailing clouds of incense.

Presently, across the road from the temple, the empty stage for thanking the gods with offerings became loud with the thunder of drums announcing the start of the folk-opera show.

Grandmother took Li-li's hand in hers and stopped at the roadside. "Li-li, do you remember the ghost last night?"

"Uh-huh," he said. "Was it Uncle Ah-ch'ing?"

"Oh, so you know? Yes, he's hiding in the air-raid shelter. Wait until there are no people about and give him this money."

"Do you want him to come back and help eat the offerings?"

"I want him to hide a little farther away," Grandmother said. "Tell him I said he's not to come back again."

"I understand," Li-li said. "Tell him not to come back again."

47

April Fools

Walking to school, Mother and I met several sixth graders coming our way. One student cried out that the bridge on the route to school was damaged, so no one need go to school today. On hearing this, the students began cheering and turned around to go home. Both Mother and I felt something was strange. Then, one student, unable to contain himself any longer and holding his sides, burst into laughter. "April Fools! Today is April Fools' Day," he said.

Later, two sixth graders came running toward us, looking terrified, and cried out, "Run everybody! Run fast! Everybody run! A mad dog is coming!" Everyone laughed, but before we knew it, a big German Shepherd came bounding around the corner. We all took off running.

This year's April Fools' Day was very interesting.

48

Rice Fields

The newspaper says that yesterday afternoon Communist bandits fired thirty-one shells toward Kinmen. None hit. Because today is the beginning of spring vacation, Mother wants to take me to Ilan to see Grandma.

We took the express train just after 2:00 p.m. Because of rain on the tracks, the train couldn't make it up a steep grade. It backed down and then tried again with more speed, but still couldn't make it. This advance and retreat went on a dozen times without success. Finally, the train returned to the station switchyard where a second locomotive was attached. The combination of the two engines finally powered the train to the top of the hill.

Our train had already been running half an hour late. Grandma and Little Uncle, who were waiting at the Ilan station for us, knew this, but they didn't know that we were now going to be more than an hour late. Mother worried about Grandma.

When we finally arrived, Mother and Grandma rode in a pedicab. I rode with Little Uncle on his bicycle. It was getting dark fast, but we were still able to see the shiny rain-washed rice fields that went on and on to the horizon.

I hoped that tomorrow I'd be playing in those fields.

As we entered the bamboo groves around the village, the two family dogs, from far off, ran barking and yelping to welcome us. I knew they had good intentions because they were wagging their tails.

Grandpa was all smiles when he saw me.

At supper I ate a big chicken leg.

49

Tea Tins

Because the swaying and jerking of the train had made me tired, I went to bed early last night. In the morning the noise of the rain woke me and dashed all my hopes to play outside. The weather was very chilly, so I wrapped up in my quilt and went back to sleep. At that time, the sky was still pitch dark, but roosters were already crowing in the near village and those beyond. Mother and Grandma still lay in bed talking. I don't know if they had just awakened, or if they had talked all night. Later I woke again. The sun had already been up for some time, and they were no longer in the house.

Everyone had finished breakfast when I came to eat. At Auntie's invitation (this is Big Uncle's wife),[45] I sat down and ate breakfast alone. From the window, I could see farmers in bamboo rain hats busy in the fields.

The village is made up of traditional houses with courtyards in the center and rooms on three sides. With the largest families, the three-sided structure might be surrounded by one or more additional three-sided structure. The village is surrounded by thriving groves of bamboo. Because the houses are so close together, I can go through doors and passages under the cover of the eaves to explore and to visit Mother's near relatives. One time I met up with a lot of my relations, both old and young. It was quite wonderful.

At lunch Grandpa took his chopsticks and served me another chicken drumstick. Actually, I'm already tired of them. Grandpa also showed me two tea tins filled with cookies and candy.

Mother and Grandma were apparently so tired that they took a long noon nap. I sat in the living room and read through several issues of the magazine *Literary World*. Before dusk, I also read a foreign story.

50

Dear Aunt

Today is Children's Day, but it's raining. I still can't go into the fields to play. This is doubly disappointing.

Mother took Grandma shopping to buy some material for making clothes.

I read two stories in *Literary World*. One of them I totally didn't understand. The other was about a farm woman and a man who went into the fields together to kiss. Very strange. If she was in her room kissing her husband, or went to the fields with him, it wouldn't have been a big deal. But she kissed the other man, and the other man had a lung disease. In the story he coughs up blood twice. Yuck!

Really bored, I went again through the passages and gates under cover of the eaves to look around. One small friend showed me his pet turtle. I really want one. Several families seem very un-usual. Their houses are small and look rundown. Inside, all have rooms with foot-operated machinery where the women weave grass rope. I never thought our family on Mother's side included such poor people.

After work Second Uncle brought back a newspaper. By chance I saw an advertisement announcing that a student bookstore in Taipei is publishing *The Children's Encyclopedia*. Forty educators wrote the books and thirty famous artists illustrated them in a Chinese edition. Each book of the set sells for NT$30. From today until the fifteenth of the month, anyone who wants to reserve a set should write to the following address: East Road, Section 1, No. 150.

I asked Mother if I could order and she said yes and suggested I write a letter to my aunt in Taipei to ask her to help handle it.

I had never written a letter before, so I found a book with some information on letter writing and read it. I asked Mother which salutation was better: Most Respectful Aunt or Dear Aunt. Mother said Dear Aunt is fine. I have a deep affection for my Dear Aunt.

Father, driving a jeep, arrived to take us home. Because driving a jeep is so convenient, Grandma gave us lots of homemade soybean cheese, pickled cucumbers, dry radishes, and similar things. Thinking our car was still not full, she found room to add some cabbage, squash, and leeks.

It was raining hard when we left, but Grandma was reluctant to let Mother go. Taking her umbrella, she walked out to the bamboo border of the village and stood on the rice paddy path. She never stopped waving. When the car turned a corner and Grandma's image disappeared, Mother couldn't keep from crying.

Because of all the rain, this trip to the countryside was disappointing. Happily, Little Uncle gave me a turtle.

Today is Tomb-Sweeping Day.[46] Returning home by way of the coastal highway, we saw many people along the roadside and in the hills cleaning the tombs of their ancestors.

"Get off when you see Keelung Harbor. The train station is right there. You remember the train station? Sure you do. It's the black building with the pointed tower," Li-li's father said.

When the Japanese withdrew from the island, they left behind the wooden train station they had constructed. The station's high Gothic-style bell tower resembles those wonderful foreign buildings printed on Christmas cards. Because it was painted with an oil varnish, the entire outside of the structure is dark.

Li-li, in fact, didn't have the vaguest idea as to the location of the train station. He only recalled that when a large number of travelers crossed over from one station platform to another on the high and enclosed wooden bridge, their footsteps made a heavy, dull, disorderly sound. This noise, which tended to linger dimly in the air, echoing off the wooden walls, was more or less Li-li's only impression of the train station. It was a very vivid impression even though the sound of the footsteps had been muffled.

In the music room at school, as he gazed absentmindedly at the black piano, he often recalled the strange sound of the footsteps and thought of when the low-tone piano keys were played.

"Are you sure he can take the train alone so far?" asked his mother. "Aren't you worried he'll get lost? He's only a fourth grader. Is he ready for this kind of training?"

"There's no need to be nervous," Li-li's father said. "He's smart enough. Li-li, are you afraid? You see. He's not afraid. Really, there's nothing to be worried about. He only needs to know exactly where he is and where he wants to go."

Li-li had long ago forgotten the image of his parents waving farewell outside his bus window, but he was still sitting rigidly erect rather than reclining in his seat. His eyes were fixed out the window. The bus passed through residential areas, where the buildings were of all heights and sizes, and it sped by sprawling markets and commercial shops. On both sides of the bus, movie-like scenes appeared, slipped alongside the bus, and then receded. Some of these scenes were part of the route which Li-li took every day to school. Other sections of the road were unfamiliar to him. But by now he had ceased to worry about missing Keelung Harbor or the train station.

The bus proceeded along Chungshan Road and, from over the top of a fence running parallel to the road, Li-li clearly saw the pointed tower of the train station. He heard the steam whistles of ships and trains. A passenger called out, "After we cross the high bridge, we'll be at the train station," and Li-li sighed with relief and leaned back in his seat. From his knapsack he pulled out a comic book to read.

It looked like it was going to rain. The entire sky was a uniform pale gray, and out in the harbor the crests of black waves broke into white foam. The ships near shore rolled with the waves and seemed to Li-li to rock like cradles. It was the first time he had come so far alone, and the new panoramic harbor view was like a painting before him.

When he stepped off the bus, he stood at the railing by the wharf, appreciating the seascape a moment. A black sea eagle circled high in the air. It flew out of the harbor and soared above the near mountains, then disappeared. Li-li began to walk toward the train station.

Pedicabs and buses passed through the narrow streets. Occasionally, the clear bell of a pedicab rang out. Bus engines grunted and groaned like fat pigs. In the arcaded street, Li-li didn't see many travelers, but in the doorway of a bar stood several American sailors, joking. Just then a southbound train pulled in. Inside, the station was quiet and deserted, except for three travelers, one janitor, and a beggar. The passengers sat on long wooden benches, staring vacantly or reading newspapers. The janitor was sweeping up cigarette butts and paper refuse from the floor. Li-li could see the beggar in the distance limping toward him.

(Grandmother will give me plenty of pocket money.)

He took the smallest coin from his pocket and dropped it into the beggar's cup. It barely made a sound, but the beggar blessed him fervently. Li-li appreciated that. This semester he placed second in his class, and he wanted to be number one. He had grown three centimeters, and he wanted to grow up to look like a cowboy in the westerns or a hero in an epic movie about Rome.

(Then Tai Chin-ch'ang wouldn't dare to make fun of me again. I'd really like to sock him, or use judo to throw him on the ground. Unfortunately, I'm not tough enough to punch him and I don't know any judo.)

He bought his train ticket, then went to wait for the train by the ticket collector's window. From a gap in a barricade, Li-li could see two large empty station platforms and several tracks. He stared at a coal-black locomotive. The isolated engine was idle, but it seemed on the verge of leaving the station. White puffs of steam came from the roof of the engine like the breath of a great beast.

The travelers gradually rose and formed a line behind Li-li. The line kept growing.

After a while, with a long sharp whistle, another coal-black engine pulling a line of black passenger cars burst in beside the station platform. The faces of tired strangers were visible in the windows, and steam swirled around the cold bright string of moving wheels. He suddenly heard the disorderly rumbling of heavy feet as the passengers poured from the cars. They flowed across the station platform and went over the wooden bridge that seemed to float in the air. Suddenly, a loudspeaker announced that the northbound train had arrived and that tickets were being taken for the east-line train. A moment later, the sounds of people calling to each other, the confusion of footsteps, and the announcements and music from the loudspeaker created a din within the station.

(What platform is the train to Ilan?)

When he came to the ticket collector, he wanted to ask him. (I ought to say, "Please, the train to Ilan.") But because he was shy, he could not utter a word. As a result, he was pushed onto the platform by the travelers behind him. Soon, enveloped by the crowd, he was swept along to he knew not where. He panicked, remembering the feeling of being lost that he had once known when separated from his mother as they hurried to catch a train. The memory made him queasy. Even when he had found the platform and boarded the passenger car, he was still nervous.

(This train, does it really go to Ilan? I ought to ask someone.) But he couldn't even ask the friendly looking young woman seated next to him. After hesitating, he finally sat down and stared dumbly out the window.

Not long after, Li-li spotted a bus traveling on the road. He could see only the top of it over the fencing along the railroad tracks. The bus pulled up for a moment at a bus stop, then resumed its normal speed, continuing up a hill. Following its movement, Li-li's eyes were led to the mountains and hills that encircled the harbor, their several shades of green now all but darkened. Suddenly, the rain began, striking the window at a slant. As the drops came harder and faster, Li-li's view of the scene was blurred.

"Little man," the friendly looking woman said as the train gradually began to move. "Where are you going all alone?"

Li-li had just taken the train schedule from his knapsack. There was a pencil inside the schedule. "I'm going to Ilan to see my grandmother. Does this train go to Ilan?"

"Yes, it does. What grade are you in?"

"I'll be a fifth grader when school starts."

"Traveling alone, do you know how to get off at the right stop?"

He nodded his head confidently, a little pride showing. Opening the train schedule all the way, he said, "I can read every station sign we reach." Then, carefully looking at the list of station names in the schedule, he added, "When I reach Toucheng I get ready to get off the train."

The woman nodded appreciatively. "That's a very clever way to do it."

As the train shot past a railroad crossing, it gave a clear warning whistle and left the suburbs, speeding into a mountain valley.

"Sitting on this side we can see the ocean," the woman said.

"Yes," he replied. "I remember that. It's why I chose to sit here. When I see Turtle Island, I'm almost to Ilan."

"You're a bright boy."

He blushed a little and his mood rose. He felt he would

never again worry about getting lost. (But I depended half on luck. I really wasn't so clear about the right platform. Although I did find the right way to the train station by myself, I ought to have asked the ticket collector, or someone else, about the right platform. That way I wouldn't have gotten scared. I actually guessed and just went with the others to this car. It gave me a cold sweaty feeling.)

Li-li sighed and relaxed. (Next time I'll know.)

With a loud noise, the train entered a tunnel. There were reflections on the windows of the car. He saw his own face and the woman's. She had pretty eyes and was wearing a soft embroidered lace collar.

"Do you know how many tunnels we pass through before Ilan?" the woman asked.

"Three," he said. "We pass through three and then can see the ocean."

"I think that's right. You really are a bright child," she said. "Which school do you go to?"

"Kuang Hwa."

"Oh, Kuang Hwa, that's a good school. I teach fourth grade at Chung Hsin."

"Chung Hsin, they beat us one time," he said. "Their dodgeball team beat ours. It made us cry, but our principal said we were really brave. In our whole school there are only twelve classes. Your school has forty-eight classes and more students, but every year we win the music competition."

"Your school's music and fine arts program is regarded very highly and is quite well-known."

"I can read music."

He could easily see the sign of the Patu station. It was above the platform in black letters on a white background. Just as the train pulled into the station, he looked through the window to the sign directly opposite him. He opened the train schedule and, at the place where it said Patu Station, he made a check with his pencil. Then he looked at his watch and said, "The train is three minutes late."

When the train stopped at Nuannuan Station, he became a little confused and apprehensive because this time his window faced out on the road and the Keelung River, so he was unable to see the station sign.

"Don't worry," the teacher said, pointing to the train schedule. "This is the station. You actually don't need to see the sign. This kind of ordinary train stops at every station. So every time it stops at a station, you just check it off. Naturally, though, you must pay attention. Sometimes, because of two trains arriving at the station at the same time, one of the trains won't stop in the station. So you still must get up and walk about until you can find the station sign. The sign is always above the station platform, and sometimes the station name is on a fence. But don't worry, until Fulung you can completely relax. I'll still be on the train. At Fulung station I get off to also go visit my grandmother. Your grandmother certainly must adore you."

"That's true," Li-li said. "She keeps a big tin box full of cookies and candy, and every day she gives me pocket money. My grandpa also loves me and my big uncle, too. I also have a young uncle who can catch fish and birds and dragonflies."

"That sounds fun."

"He even catches turtles."

The two talked on. Finally, the teacher, her head first tilting to one side several times, fell asleep.

The train shook and swayed in the rain as it passed through the mountain valley. The landscape of dense shrubs and trees and clouded mountains resembled a painting that just kept unscrolling.

At the base of one mountain, a river flowed smoothly and deeply, but where it became shallow, boulders caused the water to leap and turn white with a roar.

As the train traveled along, the scene darkened. The houses and train station were stained with black soot and coal dust, resembling a pile of discolored wooden building blocks.

"Box lunches! Box lunches!" cried a hawker, running along one side of the station platform.

His voice woke the teacher and she raised her head and looked out the window at two large piles of coal. "We must be in Juifang," she said.

"The train just stopped," Li-li said. He was viewing with curiosity two bare-backed men in the distance. Their bodies were completely caked with coal dust. They looked like demons who had just arrived from the underworld.

"Who are those men?"

"They're miners," she said. "They dig coal inside the earth. That's the coal that they bring up. Their kind of work is very dangerous, pitifully so. It's a good reason everyone should study hard when young."

"This past semester I finished second in my class," Li-li said. "I was just two points behind."

But Li-li really didn't feel happy. The view of a sky full of gray clouds, rain, and coal dust weighed on his mood. As the train began to pull away from the station, the hawkers chased after it on the platform, calling out. They reminded him of the pictures of musicians in their black costumes that hung in his school's music room.

Further along, the train crossed a steel bridge over a mountain stream and then entered a long tunnel and a shorter one. From the window there were no new or interesting views.

"In just a moment, we'll be able to see the ocean," the teacher exclaimed.

"Will you be getting off the train?" Li-li said, looking at his schedule. "The next station is Fulung."

"Yes, I will, but I know you'll have a safe trip to Ilan. Your method of using the train schedule is a good one. You really are a very intelligent boy."

After she got off the train, she came around to Li-li's window, tapped on it, and gave him the thumbs-up sign. But suddenly Li-li grew nervous again. As the train left the station, he also discovered that the passenger car was only half as full as before. He counted the unchecked station names remaining on the train schedule, looked at his watch, and realized he still had nearly half the trip to go.

(Time goes slowly. But time can also go fast. Time is strange.)

Through the window, the view of the boundless Pacific Ocean began to make him think of home. Watching the wind-driven waves, he thought of his classmates and neighborhood friends. During summer vacation they always formed teams to play ball at the school grounds or went to the harbor or woods to play.

(This afternoon they were to go swimming. But because of the rain, they are probably sheltered under some big rock.) He could picture, though, their small naked bottoms as they swam together in the sea. The thought made him smile.

(But Father doesn't like me to play all day with them. He likes me to play outdoors in the countryside. He surely has his reasons, but I don't understand. Why don't my classmates like going to the countryside? Perhaps they have no place to go in the countryside.)

Outside the window, a car or two passed occasionally on the road that paralleled the railroad tracks. The road lacked interest for Li-li, and the gray sea, dark rain clouds, and humid interior air made him sleepy.

(I should keep awake.) He sat up straight and shook his head several times. (This time I really didn't do so well. I hurried on the platform and was pushed by the crowd of people and ended up in this car, although it was the right train. But I really wasn't aware of what I was doing. It was half luck.)

He looked around the car. Some of the passengers had drooped their heads, lulled to sleep by the sound of the electric fans on the ceiling of the car.

(Time goes so slow. I still can't see Turtle Island.)

Indeed, much time had elapsed, and Li-li still hadn't caught sight of the island. Time seemed to stand still as he waited. Gradually, he, too, was lulled to sleep by the hum and click of the fans.

Asleep, he dreamed of a gray water buffalo eating grass in a lush field. He could distinctly see the tongue of the beast and its grinding *teeth. Using its tongue, it rolled up the tender shoots of grass and audibly chewed them, then swallowed.*

At the edge of the field, he saw several figures with black faces like those of religious idols. These beings, either seated or standing, after a moment bared their teeth, brandished their claws, and rushed toward Li-li. Terrified, he ran to catch a moving train. The train was enshrouded in a white mist and just that moment was speeding along-side the platform station. He vaguely heard the loudspeaker say, "Ilan. Ilan. Departing passengers please cross over the bridge."

He rolled his eyeballs but could not open his eyelids. He could only hear the muffled footsteps of the passengers crossing the wooden flyover.

As he slept, the train crossed a large bridge over a river, and Li-li could feel the rumbling sensation made by the wheels. An urgent blast of the train whistle woke him with a start.

Outside the foggy window, he could not see the ocean, only field upon field of flooded rice paddies and the farmhouses of distant villages. As had been true throughout the journey, he could still see the slanting rain.

(I must have fallen asleep) He wiped the sweat caused by the humidity from his face and looked at his watch. (I've overslept.)

He again bent over his train schedule to count the station names. The train continued flying along in the blinding rain.

(There's no reason to be afraid. I should stay calm. At the next station I'll get off and board a train going the other way. Father said, "There's no need to be afraid. You only have to know exactly where you are and where you want to go.")

American Warship

The commander of the American Seventh Fleet, Vice Admiral Griffin, will visit our country. His flagship, the USS *St. Paul*, has been anchored in Keelung Harbor for three days, and today and tomorrow it will be open to tourists.

Our family planned to go see the ship in the afternoon, but in the morning Hu Ling-yu telephoned to ask if I wanted to go with her and her father to tour it. As a result, our two families agreed to go together, meeting in front of the train station. Because Hu Ling-yu's father is a high-ranking Harbor Bureau official, we didn't have to wait in line to go aboard the heavy cruiser.

From the deck of the American warship, I could see two of our own country's destroyers anchored on the other side of the harbor. Our ships looked really small.

"If we had this kind of warship," Uncle Hu said, "there would be real hope of overthrowing the Communists on the mainland."

I think so, too. Then President Chiang would be an even greater man.

Father didn't say anything. I don't think he likes Americans.

53

Sakyamuni Buddha

Today commemorates the 2,504th birthday of Sakyamuni Buddha. Grandmother wanted me to go with her to the nearby Kuan Yin[47] Temple to worship the Buddha. The birthday rite of bathing Buddha's image takes place tomorrow, with observances beginning today. As we approached the temple, an endless procession of pilgrims passed along the road. On both sides beggars were seated shoulder to shoulder. Grandmother gave me a pocketful of change, but by the time I was just halfway along the route, I had already put it all in their begging bowls.

54

Closed Windows

Finally, school has begun again. After such a long vacation, I'm excited to be starting. The classrooms of the highest grade are quiet while students copy a review math test from the blackboard. Students in the lower grades, meanwhile, recite aloud from textbooks for their teachers. Different textbooks are used by different classes, and when several classes are reciting at once, it sounds like a large chorus echoing in a valley.

In the morning I usually like this kind of loud and mixed recitation and listen carefully to distinguish what text a particular class is reciting. Some time ago, I discovered by accident that the first-grade class no longer recited aloud the "ABC's"[48] and had begun reading regular textbooks. From that day on, I've often played this listening game.

Cheng Ch'ing-shan today still hasn't come to school.

When school let out, Mother and I went to see about him again, but the windows of his house were all closed up.

55

Still Life

In fine arts class we've already finished making plaster models and drawing still lifes. Today our teacher introduced us to water-color techniques by using four paintings as examples. I can see that the basic procedures and principles for doing watercolor and sketching are about the same. An outline is first sketched using very light color. Then the shading is applied to give the subject a still-life, three-dimensional aspect. Finally, the material qualities of the subject are represented, followed by revisions. The basic background color should be made a little darker so that the subject of the still life stands out.

56

Playing Sonatas

Workmen brought the piano to our home in town. Father wants me to begin practicing next week and not to stop. This won't be easy. It's not that I don't like music, but practicing the piano is really tiring. At mother's direction, I played from *Buyer's Beginning Practice Book*, but after several pages I didn't continue. This has already been going on for a long time.

"Before, if you had continued to practice," Father said over the telephone, "you would already be playing sonatas; you could be playing anything."

"But then I wouldn't have had enough time to read so many books," I said.

"Use the time you spend reading the newspaper," Father said. "What's the point of reading the newspaper in such detail anyway? Most of it's just boring."

I don't know how Father reads the newspaper, but I certainly find interesting things in it. For example, just yesterday there was a story about a man who speared a fish, then placed it in his mouth and held it there. Unfortunately, his companion said something to him at just the wrong moment, and, when the man with the fish opened his mouth to reply, the fish jumped down his throat, and the man choked to death. Of course, I don't think this example is necessarily the best. In fact, it's rather poor. But really though, the newspaper has many things it can teach us, such as all about flying saucers in outer space and the possibility of more advanced life out there.

Then there are instructions for training a pet dog, stories about Russia's man-made satellite falling out of the sky and burning up in the atmosphere, a mysterious bomb explosion in Siberia, etc., etc. Some of the news does repeat every day and doesn't change except for the names and locations. I'm thinking here of the cases of petty thieves, robbers, murderers, and men who love women.

No matter the situation, children must do what their fathers tell them, especially if what they say is reasonable. Father says that a young boy ought to try many things that challenge his abilities.

In my piano practice, I've had to start over almost from the beginning. This is because my foundation is weak, and I have forgotten how to read musical notation for the left hand. As soon as Mother reminds me, though, I understand, but it's still not easy to control my left hand.

57

Television Coming

I think I can adjust a little the way I read the newspaper. By doing so, I can save some time. Here's an example: "This is the last day of the painting exhibition of Yieh Tsui-pai." This news I don't need because I have no connection to Yieh Tsui-pai.

Here's another: "Academia Sinica[49] has verified that Confucius is 2,510 years old." This also isn't necessary to read. Confucius is so extraordinary that there's no point in paying attention to how old he is.

"The All-Province Track and Field Games have begun, and Lin Chao-tai has broken the nation's broad-jump record." This also I don't need to read about. Sports news just tells how someone runs and jumps here and there.

"Every new automaker is obligated to compensate drivers of multi-person pedicabs and help them adapt to new trades." This item I want to read because it refers to the time when pedicabs will have disappeared and taxis will have completely taken over.

I asked Mother what news she thought I should read, what news is useful to me?

Mother turned through the pages of the newspaper, not saying anything. Then, "All the news you aren't reading now and all the news that doesn't matter to you."

"But I really learn even from a little thing."

"For example?"

"For example, there was a council meeting someplace in which the council vice president and a councilman were both drunk.

During the meeting, they called each other dirty names and had a fight. One afternoon the same councilman, quite sober this time, punched the council vice president."

"Do you know what this was all about?"

"I know these councilmen are just like hoodlums."

"For the time being, I think you still should spend more time practicing the piano. You must also study painting. In the fall we can get a television set. Taiwan is about to get a television station. There's lots of news reports on television. Perhaps then you won't need to read the newspaper."

"How do you know about television coming?" I asked.

"There was a report in the newspaper today," Mother said.

I ran and got the paper. There it was: "China and Japan together are establishing a television station."

I immediately called Father and asked if he knew about our country establishing a television station in the fall. He said he didn't know and asked how I knew. I said I saw it in today's newspaper.

58

War Horse

For two days the weather has been cloudy and rainy. Everyone has been using the hallway at school to play war horse. In the morning, when several classes were taking their noon rest, the class leader, riding Chang Ta-lung, soundly defeated Tai Chin-ch'ang with Wang Hsiao-ming several times. Once, Chang Ta-lung knocked over Tai Chin-ch'ang and he fell on his back. Shamed and angered by this, Tai Chin-ch'ang said he wanted to have a ten-round fight to the death at noon.

Unfortunately, in the second round of the fight to the death, with the two riders—the class leader and Wang Hsiao-ming—pushing and pulling each other, the class leader unintentionally struck Tai Chin-ch'ang in the face and gave him a bloody nose. The class leader offered his apologies, but Tai Chin-ch'ang was so angry, he slapped the class leader hard twice, making him cry. Tai Chin-ch'ang at once grew nervous and told the class leader to stop crying. But the class leader cried even louder. So Tai Chin-ch'ang slapped the class leader hard again.

Because the sixth-grade classrooms are off the same hallway we were playing in, the class leader's second-oldest brother saw what was going on and ran over to Tai Chin-ch'ang and asked him what he thought he was doing. Tai Chin-ch'ang, who is a big kid, at first didn't look the class leader's second-oldest brother in the eye, but then he told him to shut his mouth or he'd hit him too. With this going on, no one had any fun.

59

Black and Blue

After yesterday's fighting, the class leader's big brother and several junior-high students stopped Tai Chin-ch'ang on the road after school. One of them hit him in the eye and made it swell black and blue.

60

Big Brother

Neither the class leader nor Tai Chin-ch'ang came to class today. Our teacher asked why. The assistant class leader then told what had happened. Our teacher told the students who are neighbors of the two to tell them that tomorrow they must come to class.

What happened next was that Tai Chin-ch'ang's high-school brother brought several friends with him early and beat up the class leader's big brother after stopping him on the road.

We Just Saw a Movie

Today, the class leader and Tai Chin-ch'ang came to class.

Teacher scolded the class leader, saying, "When Tai Chin-ch'ang hit you that day, why didn't you come tell me?"

The class leader began to cry and said, "I was afraid he would hit me again."

Teacher asked Tai Chin-ch'ang, "Why do you do behave this way? How can you insult and abuse a classmate and hit them like that?"

Tai Chin-ch'ang quickly responded, "His big brother with several dumb bullies hit me. So this morning my brother and several friends hit him back."

Our teacher angrily said, "This is all because you think you can just hit people as you please. And the fighting leads to more fighting until it gets completely out of control. That's the outcome."

Our teacher struck Tai Chin-ch'ang hard in the palm five times with a rattan stick. The class leader was punished with detention.

Planes were buzzing the town and dropping bombs. Everywhere houses exploded and billows of smoke and dust rolled up into the sky. A young military officer and a young woman, leading a group of orphanage children, fled into a narrow bombed-out alley.

On the movie screen the bombing ceased. Slow sad music played as the fleeing children and adults sought to console one another. The audience wept quietly.

Suddenly, a hard crackling rain hit the theater roof, startling Li-li and giving him chills. His heavy eyelids again closed, and he snuggled into the warm crook of his mother's arm and slept.

The movie ended and two ushers came down the aisles and opened the side doors of the theater.

When Li-li was awakened by the noise of the audience, a line of credits was running on the screen upon a scenic background of open sea and blue sky.

"Where is this?" he wondered aloud.

"We're in the movie house, put your coat on," his mother said. "We must go home."

The horizontal beam of the projector and the screen's bright silver light suddenly were extinguished. Everywhere in the theater bright warm lights came on and upbeat music played. People rose, banged back their seats, and left the comfortable theater by the side doors, entering a cold wind and the deep cave of night. The wind, blowing on Li-li's neck, awakened him completely as he stood with his mother in the door of the theater.

"What happened in the movie," Li-li asked. "It was raining hard. Is it still raining?"

"The rain seems to have stopped," his mother said, peering into the darkness. She took off her silk stockings from under her skirt and wrapped them around Li-li's neck inside his coat collar. "What was the last thing happening in the movie before you fell asleep?"

"The bad guys had entered the city."

"The movie was almost over by then," Li-li's mother said, "That young officer later died and so did the woman. The children took a boat to another place."

"Oh."

"The story was too sad; next time we'll come and see The Happy Garden in a Corner of the Sea. The preview looked very interesting. Now let's go home."

But Li-li's brain was still full of the images of houses exploding and dust and smoke billowing skyward as the bombs of the air raid devastated the town. He remembered also the rain hitting the theater roof, making him tremble and feel chilled.

Street lamps lit up the wet surface of the road, but not a drop of rain was still falling. From every drain and gutter, runoff was pouring into the streams and creeks that emptied into the harbor. In several places beneath the lights of ships, waves from the blackness of the sea swung up into the light, shone, and disappeared.

Shops with neon signs were already closed. Only the scattered lights of food stalls and the dim street lamps gave an outline to the business district. Li-li and his mother, leaving the crowd around the movie house, took a shortcut and entered an alleyway. In the daytime this alley was a vegetable market lined with stalls and stall keepers.

Inside the arcade were clothing stores, a grocery, and other retail shops. Given the gloom of the night sky and the distance of the street lamps, it was intensely dark inside the arcade where they walked. An offensive smell of fish and meat broth permeated the cold air.

"You ____ mother ____!" an angry voice suddenly cried from the darkness. Out in the street a flashlight clicked on, throwing light on a youth wearing a cotton T-shirt and pajama bottoms. He was being pulled by the hair and forced head down on a meat butcher's counter.

Startled, Li-li's mother froze and clutched Li-li tightly to her. Pressed against the softness of his mother's breasts, he could feel her body trembling and hear the rapid beating of her heart.

When the flashlight was extinguished, Li-li, in the depths of his heart, struggled to comprehend what was happening. The man pulling the hair of the youth grasped a broad, shining butcher knife in his free hand. Li-li shivered just as he had when the heavy rain had suddenly hit the roof of the theater. From out of the darkness came the click of a cigarette lighter followed by the glow of three cigarette tips.

"It's already late," a low and heavy voice said. Then coldly, "You can send him straight to hell."

The flashlight again shone on the meat counter and the pallid face.

"If you don't want to talk, then you must not want to live."

The eyes of the man with the pale face were still open, but they were expressionless. His tiny open mouth said nothing, only took in air in gasps. He appeared stunned and paralyzed like a fish out of water.

"You really won't talk? All right." The man speaking turned off the flashlight. "You get an express trip to hell. Do it!"

The sound of chopping blows came from the meat stall. Li-li's back was hurting where his mother held him tightly. He felt her body jerk hard.

When the two of them opened their eyes, the men were already gone.

"Let's go home fast," Li-li's mother said breathlessly. "We must quickly leave here, Li-li."

In the distance, the noise of a police siren approached. Several lights in nearby apartment windows went on. Some people stayed be-

hind their windows, moving about, while others came out to investigate.

Li-li and his mother hurried down an alley to escape.

The police car came up alongside them and stopped. One policeman stuck his head out of the car window. "What are you doing?"

Li-li's mother was too frightened to speak.

"We're just on our way home," Li-li said. "We just saw a movie and now we're going home."

62

Flight Home

Thailand's commander-in-chief of the air force and eighteen staff persons ended a visit to our country yesterday afternoon. On their flight home today, the plane struck Wuchih Mountain in Taipei, killing all aboard. The distinguished guests had come from very far away and now will never return home. It really is a huge embarrassment.

American Navy scientists successfully launched the Polaris ballistic missile from deep in the sea. This kind of missile is installed on nuclear submarines and can carry nuclear warheads. Recently, America has brought out many new things: satellites, space rockets, and air-to-air interceptor missiles.

My country has some important successes, too. In Taipei, a seven-story building was recently completed. The newspaper says Taiwan Cement Company's new concrete building is more than one hundred feet tall, just a little lower than the Presidential Palace. It's the biggest structure built in Taiwan since recovery of the island from Japan. In addition to air conditioning, it has elevators so office workers don't have to climb the stairs.

63

New Park

Mother took me to my Taipei aunt's home to ask her to advance order the *Children's Encyclopedia*. Auntie was very happy when she saw me. We last saw her on Chinese New Year. She refused to take Mother's deposit money. She said her nephew is like a son.

Before going to Auntie's house, Mother took me to the district near the Taipei train station and Tungfang book store to buy several books. The store is filled with children's books. I like it very much. Mother says in the future we can go there once each month to find books that we can't find or borrow in the library.

Later we arrived at New Park and took a walk inside. It was strange. In an old restored locomotive, I found a cotton quilt and some clothing. Auntie laughed about this and said that New Park is a hotel and godown for idlers. She went on to mention some of the strange and dangerous things that go on in the park: In the early morning some people practice martial arts, trampling and ruining the grass at the same time. One person was seen practicing "steel legs," and he actually kicked over a young coconut tree. At dusk, there's always gambling, including gambling for cigarettes, and there's fortune-telling. You can also buy curious medicated plasters attached to pieces of paper or cloth. People are always sitting with their legs crossed and blocking the entrance to the park. Hoodlums grab people off the street, including tourists, and trick them into gambling at their stalls. At the same time, some of them strong-arm people to pay gambling debts or protection money. These people always come and go at the park's entrance and fool around with the revolving gate. Some adults take over the children's playground equipment. And some have even been known to kidnap children who are playing there. Young women should not go in the park, especially in the evening. More than a few sex fiends hang out there, says Auntie.

64

Taking Poison

For several days the weather has been all rain, clouds, and cold, owing to the typhoon. This has everyone depressed. No wonder the newspaper says that, according to annual statistics, the most suicides on the island occur in the months of March, April, and September.

The suicide rate is highest among poor people, such as workers, farmers, fishermen, seamen, clerks, office or errand boys, apprentices, mailmen, barbers, drivers, pedicab operators, peddlers, cooks, and other menial laborers. Each year an average of 125 persons in these groups commit suicide.

Marital problems—including quarrels, desertion, maltreatment, abuse, extramarital affairs, etc.—bring on the suicide of 101 persons annually.

To be saddened by or to resent an injustice, to hate the world because of not doing well, to be discouraged over flunking a competitive exam for a job or school admission, to be cheated or swindled, disgraced, etc.—these claim the lives of seventy-three persons each year.

There's so many people who have died, it takes too much time to write down all the information about it. I've already spent too much time on it as it is. Father will surely scold me. In any event, I don't see myself committing suicide. There are students who kill themselves, but all are above junior-high level.

Methods of killing yourself include taking poison, drowning, hanging, using a knife or a gun, lying down on railroad tracks, and jumping from a building. Poisoning is probably the easiest way to go, but drowning is also popular because Taiwan has water on all sides as well as many rivers. But there was one pair of lovers who jumped into a river and found it too cold to bear, so they got out and walked away.

Very few jump from buildings, because in Taiwan there are so few tall ones. Jumping from most buildings would accomplish very little.

The Tree that Blossoms with White Flowers

The newspaper reports that a year-and-half-old girl, in the middle of the night, while her parents were sleeping, climbed to the edge of the bed, fell into the chamber pot and drowned. I asked mother why there are families that have chamber pots in the bedroom. Mother said many country families have this custom, and the chamber pots are later emptied to fertilize the fields.

The province really has many strange goings-on: One farmer was rebuilding his house with the help of his son. The old farmer doesn't know if it was his poor vision and the late light of day or his own carelessness, but whatever it was, he wanted to drive a nail into a post and drove it instead into his son's skull, killing him.

One worker in a brick foundry was being pestered by a fly. The worker sprayed his own feet with insecticide and then sprayed the bodies of two oxen in the factory as well. One ox licked itself all over and suddenly pitched over and died. This startled the other ox which then kicked and ran away. Unfortunately the workman became tangled in the reins and was dragged along the ground by the ox. Some workmen tried to help out, but by the time they got to him he was already critically injured and couldn't be revived.

A hunter took his gun up the mountain to go hunting. On the mountain slope he saw a naked corpse. He ran down the mountain to a branch office of the police and got a policeman to come and see. Who would have thought they'd find only an old man with his clothes off, sunbathing.

On this holiday morning, village children of all ages gathered on the tree-bordered vacant lot, playing card games or shooting marbles. They liked to play these games with Wang Hsin-piao. With him playing, it was always exciting because he either won big or lost big. On this morning, he had already won enough paper cards to fill three pillowcases, and enough marbles to almost fill a water bucket.

"Come here, Li-li," said Wang Hsin-piao, standing just outside the trees and waving his hand. "I want to talk with you. I have some-

thing to tell you."

Li-li left the circle of children playing card games and followed after Wang Hsin-piao.

"Do you want to go somewhere, Ah-piao?" Li-li said.

"I want to go find my father," Wang Hsin-piao said. "He went into the mountains. I saw him last month go into the mountains."

"What did he go into the mountains for?"

"I don't know," said Wang Hsin-piao, sniffling. "He went somewhere in the mountains."

Quietly, he took a few steps, then his eyes filled with tears and he said, "Next school term I won't be going to class. I won't be studying again. Anyway, my homework is terrible. What's six times eight? I don't know. Seventy-two?"

"Six times eight is forty-eight. But you should think more about your successes."

"Who cares. I'll go learn to be a carpenter. In my house we have plenty of tools. I can earn money and then go gamble and win more. I can win a lot of money. I don't want to be like my father and older brother. They always lose. They're very, very unlucky."

———————————

"The son of Mrs. Wang, the woman who helps wash clothes, has been arrested again by the police," Li-li's mother said.

"Wasn't he just let out of jail?" Li-li's father asked.

"He's been out for several days. I hear he's been acting strange. On the second day home, he rushed out to find a job as a brick carrier. He said he wanted to learn cement work, but it probably was too hard for him. A few days later, he went to the grocery store to buy a bottle of rice wine and some cigarettes. He said he wanted to buy them on credit, but the woman proprietor wouldn't let him. This woman, by the way, is actually just a little...well, difficult herself. He probably said something bitter to her. The two of them argued, and some people who heard them shouting came to the store. The result was that in the middle of the night on the same day, the police came and arrested him."

"Did he hit someone?"

"No, but probably—because he felt disgraced—he was angry

enough to say something he regrets. Other people reported him to the police. The washerwoman truly is in a tough situation. I've heard that her husband's also gone, the carpenter."

"Perhaps he's been arrested by the police at his gambling haunt."

"Usually a person can find out about such things. At least contact someone," the mother said. "But in this case there hasn't been even a little news."

"Ask the neighborhood chief or the community chief."

"She already pleaded with them to go to the police station and inquire, but nothing," the mother said. "This woman's situation is just awful. She has no men at home now. Yesterday their landlord's wife and son fought with her and gave her a black eye. She's two months behind in the rent. The neighborhood chief's wife also is a bit too much. They rent out illegal houses to two families at the same time. I've also heard that a single man, a miner, violated the daughter."

"Whose daughter?"

"The daughter of the washerwoman. The miner comes from mainland China. He's not what you call high class. Otherwise he would have married her and made do with what they had. That way all could have been forgotten. But now the girl's caught up in this sad drama, and she's terrified. What a pity, and only fifteen years old."

"All right, that's enough," Li-li's father said. "The more you tell me, the more tragic and pathetic it sounds."

At the edge of the village, the two boys took the small road on which Wang Hsin-piao's house was located and dropped down to a river valley; then they climbed up to another village built for government employees. The houses here were built in neat and orderly rows. In all parts of the village, children were playing together in clean lanes and alleys.

"Where are you going?" a classmate who recognized them asked. "Li-li?"

Li-li hesitated. "We're going to climb the mountain," he said finally.

"That's great," a classmate said. "We'll go with you."

Another said, "Just wait a moment while I go put on some shoes."

"We aren't going for fun," Wang Hsin-piao said with some force and rudeness. "We have something we need to do."

"What could you possibly have to do on the mountain?" a stout, muscular youth said. "You must be going just for fun."

"We're not. It's not a fun thing at all," Li-li said.

"You're putting us on. If you're going to climb the mountain, how come you're wearing sandals?"

"It's none of your business if we wear sandals," Wang Hsin-piao said. "If someone wears sandals, why can't they climb a mountain?"

"If you were climbing the mountain barefoot, I'd believe you."

"Goddamn you. Sandals or barefoot, what's it to you?" Wang Hsin-piao said. "We'll climb our mountain and you can go climb yours." "I'm sorry," Li-li said to his classmates. "Next time I'll certainly go climbing with you. But this time, we really can't do it." He looked back at Wang Hsin-piao. "That's how it is, right, Ah-piao?"

Wang Hsin-piao nodded and looked away. His proud attitude angered several of the boys. One of the leaders cursed Wang Hsin-piao loudly and pushed him. The two threw several punches, one striking Wang Hsin-piao in the mouth and knocking a tooth out.

"You've given me something to remember," Wang Hsin-piao said, spitting blood on the ground. Pointing at his attacker, he said, "My older brother will come back and then we'll see where you can run to."

"Your older brother got arrested again," the classmate said. "And besides I also have an older brother."

"I'll go to our teacher and say you are hitting people," Li-li said.

"I'm not afraid," the classmate said. "During summer vacation there are no teachers."

"My father will come and have a talk with your father."

"My father…when my father knows, I'll beat you up for sure."

"Let's go, Li-li," Wang Hsin-piao said. "I'll settle this with him later."

They continued through the village and came to the foot of a small mountain. Two bulldozers, halfway up the slope, were busy moving dirt. The mountain was being cut in half and leveled to build a middle school. Across the mountainside a narrow road had been cut through native trees and grasses and was being used to open up and develop more land on the mountain. On the backside of the mountain, demolition operations were being carried out in another hollow. Every once *in a while an explosion would shower rocks and dust into the air.*

Wang Hsin-piao, head down, was concentrated on climbing the mountain road when Li-li said, "Where are we going? They're blasting on the mountain in front of us." Just as he finished saying this, another explosion threw rubble and dust into the distant sky.

"We haven't got far to go," Wang Hsin-piao said. "We only have to go up ahead to that burial ground."

"Huh? What are we going to do at a burial ground?" Li-li asked.

"This is where we'll find my father. The day I saw him, he was just entering it."

"From there, though, wouldn't he have gone someplace else?"

"What other place? He couldn't go anywhere else," Wang Hsin-piao said. "He owes people money, a lot of money. Hoodlums came to see him several times. They want to kill him."

"Since it's a burial ground, we ought to have more people with us. We should find lots of other people to come with us."

"You needn't be afraid. I can go in by myself if you like, and you can stay here and wait for me."

"I...I'll go with you."

There was black mud everywhere on the desolate, weedy grounds, and the air was filled with a stale and moldy smell like that of a basement. But when the wind blew gently through the trees, their leaves reflecting sunlight, the two boys could smell the fragrance of flowers.

"What flower smells so good?" Wang Hsin-piao asked.

"It's a gardenia," Li-li said. "You have this kind of tree behind your house. It's a tree that blossoms with white flowers."

"It blossoms with white flowers, I know. I saw it." Then, squinting with his near-sighted eyes, Wang Hsin-piao said, "Is that a tree in front of me? It looks like there's a man standing under it. Is it my father? It looks like my father!"

"Oh, Ah-piao. It is your father," Li-li said. "But he seems to be hanging there, not standing."

66

Coal Dust

On the way to school, out the window of the public bus, I saw Cheng Ch'ing-shan. He was with several women who live in the neighborhood. They were bent over at the side of the road, using their hands to recover coal mud from the ditches. Every time the factory's coal-washing section is drained, the coal dust washes into the drainage ditches. At the sides of the ditches, or at special places, layers of coal mud form. This attracts lots of people seeking to reclaim it. They take the coal mud home and pile it in an open space. When enough is collected, they divide it among themselves. Then the material is rubbed into balls. They use wood to burn these coal balls, and then they bury them in the ground. In time they are changed into refined charcoal. Finally, the charcoal is taken to town to sell.

67

Like a Beehive

It has continued to rain for several days. Water is in all the low-lying areas, and mud and sand, too, so there's no way to do any cleanup work. At school, the leaves of the trees are scattered far and wide, and in all the flower gardens it's surprising how much grass has sprung up.

Forgetting the rain for a while, we boys played war horse in the hallways, and the girls jumped rope and played a juggling game called little rice bag. Those who did not join in talked in groups or just goofed around. When classes were over, the inside of the school buzzed and hummed like a beehive.

I still was a little concerned that with more hard rain, this very small wooden school might actually collapse and become part of the weeds.

68

On the Sly

During the noon rest period,[50] Lin Te-sheng spoke to me on the sly. He said he had discovered a fun thing to do. I went with him. There were several students from our class already hiding at the spot, laughing and talking about what they would do. Runoff from the rains of the last several days had created a small waterfall on the mountain cliff behind the music classroom. The waterfall, in turn, formed a stream. We picked up stones and mud and made a dirt dam to change the stream's course. It no longer flowed into the drainage ditch by the side of the music room, but rather back around the ledge of another cliff to make another waterfall.

The result of this change was that the water flowed across the school grounds right toward the back windows of the teachers' offices. We immediately ran away.

In the afternoon, with first period over, all the school children suddenly thought a disaster had come. Because of the new course of the stream, the entrance to the boys' and girls' rest rooms was flooded. No one could get through.

We hydraulic engineers each received one swat on our palms from our teacher's rattan stick.

69

My Handkerchief

Today in fine arts class, we painted watercolor still lifes: three bananas, one papaya, and a pineapple. The pineapple was hard for many people to do, and most didn't even try to paint the papaya.

Teacher chose five paintings and put them up on the back wall of the classroom for everyone to see. Mine was among the five. Also, of the five top students in the first monthly exams, I am the only one who can paint. Tai Chin-ch'ang's monthly exam results were especially poor, but he still is the best painter.

After school I went with Mother to the student canteen to eat lunch and ran into Hu Ling-yu. She and a student from the Harbor Bureau were huddled at the door of the school supplies store under the eaves waiting for a bus. I hadn't talked with her for quite a while. In fact, I had nearly forgotten her. If the weather is good, I'm usually running all over the place, and I often run into her in the schoolyard somewhere. When everyone else is busy playing, she finds time to touch my face lightly or pat my back. Once she even helped me pick up my handkerchief which I had dropped as I was hurrying away.

On rainy days it's not easy to run into each other. Our classrooms aren't in the same part of the school. During the last several days, I had only caught a glimpse of her once, one hand shielding her face against the rain and the other holding up her skirt as she rushed to the teachers' offices.

"Hey, Li-li," she said happily, catching sight of me, her eyes brightening. "I haven't seen you in a long time. I hear you are practicing the piano again."

She was holding her wide-brimmed hat, and her hair and face were wet with rain. I thought she was very beautiful; her face glowed. I said nothing; I could only give her a warm smile.

"When can you come play at our house again?" Mother asked.

"Next week," she answered. "But I have to talk with Mother first."

When we said good-bye, I noticed again the fragrance on her body.

70

Opposing Candidates

Because Mother wants to cast her vote today for mayor and provincial assemblymen, we returned yesterday to our house in town.

I woke early this morning, but not to the noise of campaign cars and trucks as I expected. In this suddenly quiet atmosphere, some people will be elected, fulfilling their dreams, while others, disappointed, will lose. For the candidates, today is probably quite nerve-racking. Father says the election campaign this time for Keelung City's representative to the Provincial Assembly is very peaceful because both candidates are KMT.[51] On the other hand, the campaign for mayor of Keelung has been especially fierce, like two tigers fighting.

Yesterday evening Father took us to see a movie: *The Trial of War Criminal Tung T'iao*. I must have grown taller recently because the movie theater people said I had to buy a half ticket. I've already outgrown the free ticket.

After leaving the theater, we ate at Miao K'ou. While there, two campaign vehicles with opposing candidates for mayor drew up across from each other. Lin Po-wang, one of the candidates, claimed he had been pressured in various ways by the KMT. Li Kuo-chun, the competing candidate, immediately contradicted Lin Po-wang, and both men began arguing loudly. After a while, campaign aides even began to scuffle. Among the crowd of onlookers, some volunteered to help Lin Po-wang fight the KMT side with their bare fists. Then everyone was shocked when someone drew a gun. Fortunately, the military police arrived in time. But the person with the gun stole off in the confusion of the crowd.

Our school teachers hope we can convince our parents to support the KMT. I asked Mother if we were supporting the KMT, and she said we listen to Father. I asked Father whom we will support, and Father did not say anything. He just laughed.

The entire evening Father lay on the living-room sofa reading the novel *Dr. Zhivago* and listening to election returns on the radio.

Lin Po-wang of Keelung City and T'u Tung-fa of Pingtung County are both opposed by KMT candidates for mayor and county magistrate, respectively. Lin Po-wang finally won with fifty-one percent of the vote.

Kennedy and Nixon

At lunch time, teachers and some young workers were talking about the election results. They said that the KMT had won a great victory. KMT candidates for the Taiwan Provincial Assembly captured fifty-eight out of seventy-three seats. KMT candidates for county magistrate and mayor positions won thirty-one of thirty-three races. Although the teachers all support the KMT, not all the factory workers do. One worker jokingly asked me what party I supported. I said I didn't know, I really didn't. They also talked heatedly about the American election. Some supported Kennedy and others Nixon.

Several teachers arranged to get together at the music teacher's home for dinner. In the evening, I went with Lin Te-sheng to his home. He had invited me to visit him several times, and he said he often mentioned me to his father. He told his father we were good friends, and his father wanted me to come to their house. When I saw his father, I recognized him at once. He is a guard at the factory gate. He's big and tall and has very pale skin. His eyebrows are thick and he has large eyes. The light in his eyes is very sharp. I never expected him to be such a friendly man. Lin Te-sheng's mother is thin and small. She's the kind of person who smiles all the time.

The dinner's main course was fried beef, very tasty, but hot. I told them that the vendor who sells *ta ping*,[52] whenever he sees Lin Te-sheng coming, hides the hot pepper sauce. They had a good laugh over this.

After dinner, Lin Te-sheng took me to his room to look at several photo albums. He had five older brothers and sisters when the family lived on the mainland. He was the sixth child, but he was born in Taiwan. One of his older brothers now has a lung disease. Every month his father sends money to him through relatives in Hong Kong. Lin Te-sheng says his father originally lived in Hunan and was a county magistrate. In Taipei, Lin Te-sheng now has several uncles on both sides of the family—all in the military. When the Communist Party closed in on their home in the country, his older brothers and sisters all were away studying. His father and mother packed up and fled in the middle of the night.

When Mother came to take me home, the family and I said good-bye at the door. I also said to Mother, "Uncle[53] Lin used to be a county magistrate on the mainland."

Uncle Lin smiled and his face got red. "It was nothing, nothing. A man in a defeated army has no claim to bravery."

I thought I had certainly said something wrong.

72

Dirty Tricks

On the phone, I asked Father how Mayor Lin Po-wang could have defeated Li Kuo-shun. Father was silent a moment, then said a few things candidly to me. In my heart I secretly had to laugh. Then I told him two stories. One day Li Kuo-shun and two provincial assemblymen came to the local factory to campaign. The factory represents two thousand votes, all assumed to be pro-KMT. When they arrived, the main gate was opened and the workers gave them an enthusiastic welcome. It was also specially arranged for them to speak.

The second day Lin Po-wang came. The factory, however, didn't open its gate. Factory officials wanted him to follow the proper office procedures to gain admittance. Lin Po-wang was left waiting at the entrance in the rain. Many factory workers saw this and felt it was unfair, and they sympathized with Lin Po-wang.

"Huh!" Father said with surprise.

I also told him that I'd heard that those two provincial assemblymen, both KMT who knew they would be elected, still fought for votes in a highly negative way, using dirty tricks. They forgot that the two of them, along with Li Kuo-shun in the race for mayor, were united in a struggle against Lin Po-wang, one person. There was one candidate running for councilman who wore glasses. Everywhere voters were told to vote for the candidate who wore glasses. But because Lin Po-wang also wore glasses, some voters were confused and voted for him. They picked the councilman and they picked the mayor, both candidates who wore glasses.

"Ha, ha. How do you know all this?" Father asked.

"I read it in the newspaper."

"The newspaper is like your constant companion. Did you practice the piano today?"

"I'm just on my way to practice."

"What are you practicing?"

"A piece called `Colorado Evening.' Today in music class, our teacher taught us `Colorado Evening.'"

73

Roof Tiles Flying Like Butterflies

Yesterday a typhoon warning was announced, but today all restrictions have been removed. The clouds are racing in the sky and the rain has temporarily stopped.

Freshets and waterfalls still spill from the mountainside and cliffs by the school, but the drainage ditches are no longer overflowing.

The students of the graduating class are working to repair their flower garden, removing grass, loosening dirt, and sweeping the fallen leaves. The windows have been cleaned and made to sparkle, and then opened wide to let out the musty air of the classrooms.

I hope the rainy season[54] is over now.

Our teacher, however, says that tomorrow could still bring rain.

He was standing pressed against the window sill of a large picture window that looked out on a grape arbor entwined with branches, leaves, and rattan vines. Within the wall that surrounded the house and yard stood a grove of trees.

"What are you doing standing there, Li-li?" his mother asked. Then, more to herself than to Li-li, she murmured, "Yesterday your

103

father should have sealed that window from the outside."

The clock on the living room wall struck the hour. The radio at the same time stopped playing music and began a broadcast of typhoon developments. In live on-the-scene coverage, wet and exhausted news reporters spoke anxiously of typhoon dangers as the wind howled and roared like static in the background.

Yesterday's weather report, although speculative, had not been so threatening. It said a typhoon could reach land at Hengch'un or on the southeast coast of the island. At noon, warnings were extended to districts along the east side of the island and in the northeast. By evening, everyone believed that the typhoon's outer edge would only brush Taiwan's northeast corner. All day the sky changed back and forth between clear and cloudy, but the rain stopped. Though it poured in the night, it did not cause much concern. But as everyone slept, the typhoon—then off the coast of Keelung—first stalled, then made a turn landward gaining great velocity, and by morning had hit Taiwan with great force.

From the mountain peaks the wind and rain swarmed into the river valley; in the sky the disturbance created a patch of milky-gray revolving air like a wall or a fast-moving fog. Through the swaying and whipping branches of his yard, Li-li at the window could see down the river valley to the crowded village residences upon both banks. He could make out the irregular line of rooftops, their contrasting heights, and several brick walls. At that moment some people with wooden boards in their hands were sealing doors or windows, or securing roofs by draping ropes over them and anchoring the ends in the ground.

"You're still standing there, Li-li?" his mother said, coming through the door. She walked over to the side of the window. "With this kind of storm, I really ought to tell your father to seal it tight. Come away from there right now. Something could come flying along and break the glass."

"I see the roof of my classmate's house moving," Li-li said. "Last year the typhoon collapsed their house and killed their little daughter. She was a model student."

"That was tragic," Li-li's mother said. "But there's no use in watching. I mean it now. Come away from the window."

Putting her arm around his shoulders, she led him into the living room. Li-li's father was resting on the sofa, reading a Japanese novel.

"How long will the wind blow like this?" Li-li asked.

"It won't be over even by midnight," Li-li's father said. "I'm sure there will still be strong winds for several more hours."

"Too bad. I saw my friend's rooftop swaying and bucking."

"There's no problem with our house," his father said, listening attentively to the wind pushing and dragging on the walls. "You can stop worrying and do your homework; I notice that you haven't done any all day."

"You better fasten that door and window securely," Li-li's mother said. "We've never had this kind of wind before."

"I don't think it's a problem," Li-li's father said, burying his head in his book again.

"I see," his mother said. "Li-li, go get your homework and do it here in the living room."

"There's no way I can do any homework," Li-li said. "The sound of the wind is too scary."

"You can write a little," his father said. "Later in the evening, the electricity will go off."

"All right," Li-li said.

He returned to the room to get his writing book, but could not refrain from taking another look out the window.

In this little while, the grapevines had already been stripped from the trellis and had blown away. Some of the trees in the grove had fallen and their tangled roots and dirt wads were tipped up in the air. With the trees thinned, he was able to see all the way to the highway that passed around the village and to the mountain range beyond it. In the violent wind and rain, the mountains seemed to Li-li to be cautiously bowing and the highway creeping timidly across the landscape. Listening the whole day to the frightening sound of the wind, he gradually had begun to comprehend that one gust of wind was pushed from behind by another gust, and that the force of the wind was built up by successive, fast-moving surges. Li-li watched how the wind would tear for a moment at the roof of his classmate's house, and then in the next moment let it go.

The wind roared and thrashed and bumped, at times curling upward, at times plunging to earth. The roof tiles on many homes of the *village were being swept away layer by layer. The neighborhood was filled with the sounds of wooden walls and partitions cracking and ripping apart.*

"You were standing at that window again, weren't you?" His mother said in the living room. "Li-li?"

"My classmate's roof is going to blow off again," Li-li said. "The roof tiles are flying like butterflies."

"Even more reason why you must stay away from that window," his mother said. "Surely one of those tiles will strike the window."

"None of them hit the window last year," Li-li said.

"This year the wind is much bigger," his father said. "Do you hear me?"

"All right," Li-li said.

74

Leather Shoes

The day after tomorrow we take our second monthly exams. In the evening, Mother helped me review. There weren't any problems, so afterward we talked.

Mother asked about people in my school, what special impressions of them I had. I said that the principal, music instructor, art teacher, and gym coach all stood out in my mind. I've already studied at three schools, so I have a basis for comparison. Our short, fat principal is very friendly. She often observes our classes and likes to mingle with us on the school grounds when we're playing. One time I saw her bending over—with some difficulty—to pick up some broken glass on the playground. She must have been thinking about the many students who still go barefoot to school. Mother has a good idea in this regard. She thinks there should be a rule that all students must wear cloth shoes. She doesn't like it that some wear leather shoes and others go barefoot.

"Do you think the students who wear leather shoes hurt the feelings of their classmates?" Mother asked me. "Do you want to wear leather shoes to class or not?"

106

"I think I need to wear leather shoes because of those students who also wear leather shoes. The class leader's leather shoes, for instance, are falling apart, and he often gets laughed at because of them, but he still wears them."

Mother asked me what I could have been thinking when I and some other students built the dirt dam and flooded the rest rooms.

I think the whole thing was an accident; we really didn't want it to happen that way. Sometimes, though, I think punishment is justified, as in the case of students like Tai Chin-ch'ang. If he isn't punished, his behavior can get worse, and this can cause trouble for other students. Nonetheless, some teachers punish people in weird ways. Teacher Wu, in the classroom next to ours, likes to pinch us, and she even pinches our cheeks.

We talked about different things and finally about Hu Ling-yu. I mentioned to Mother that I smelled some fragrance on her body. Mother said perhaps it was perfumed soap. I said no. Mother's face seemed to redden. I said Hu Ling-yu's class work is very good, and she also plays the piano well, but she isn't too knowledgeable about many things; she knows only a few things.

Mother appreciated my talking about myself and Hu Ling-yu. She said that I'm already beginning to distinguish my capabilities from those of others, and this kind of understanding, she said, is very valuable.

75

One Seat

Today I got perfect scores on the exams and so did the class leader.

Because of family troubles, Cheng Ch'ing-shan can't stay in school. As a result, the students in his row all moved ahead one seat. The class leader now has become my neighbor. Last night's talk about Hu Ling-yu and me was interesting. So I compared myself to the class leader also.

Because his body is more developed than mine, he's better

than I am in sports. Father often encourages me to participate in sports. He says they can sharpen one's instincts and responses. Athletics, he says, can also build spirit by teaching one to advance in the face of difficulties and opposition—in other words, to keep going and work hard whatever the situation.

76

To Bed Early

I had all perfect scores on this month's exams, but eight other classmates had the same. Because I so recently transferred to this school, everyone treated me especially well. It seems that all at once I have won my classmates' respect and friendship, which makes the scores I got seem even higher.

Because Hu Ling-yu wasn't careful, she made a mistake on a math question and is very disappointed. She keeps repeating over and over that her luck isn't good. She seems really sad. She'd planned to come to our house to practice piano with me, but now she has no interest in practicing. After dinner, Mother urged her to take a bath and go to bed early.

"Why is she so low?" I asked Mother.

"I'm also very surprised. I've never seen her so worried and anxious," Mother said. "Maybe it's the experience of not getting a perfect score on the examination, and perhaps she is afraid her father will scold her. Are you sometimes afraid of Father?"

I told her that sometimes I'm afraid, but if Father knows I've made a mistake, I can tell him I'm sorry and right away he stops being angry. If I haven't made a mistake, I can argue the point, and he often finally agrees with me.

Whose Wife of the Seven Is She?

Mother again invited a group of students to take a walking trip, this time to Heavenly Dynasty Temple. We followed a grass path up and over a small mountain and descended the back side, passing near a village and finally reaching the temple built in a mountain valley.

Before we began to climb the mountain, we saw several of our classmates and residents of the area below the slope on a barren stretch of ground. Dust was flying up from a dumped cart-load of waste carbide powder, and the people were scurrying to pick up scrap iron and copper. Most had covered their heads and faces, as well as the rest of their bodies. Once the diluted carbide powder gets spread out, it sometimes scalds people. One time I saw kids on the lower side of our village with crippling burns on their feet. Some adults still have scars on their arms.

From the summit, we could see a small train hauling coal at the foot of the mountain. We passed by a mining village with a primary school. All of the houses there were stained with coal dust and looked dark gray.

In the temple, crowds of people were worshipping. Mother gave every student a joss stick. We lined up behind the worshippers to offer our prayers. In no time at all the large temple hall was filled with clouds of incense smoke.

Hu Ling-yu said with regret that if she had come to pray one week earlier, perhaps she wouldn't have missed the arithmetic problem. I can respect the gods, but last year I accompanied grandmother to Kuan Yin Temple before my exams, and I still didn't get a perfect score. I had clearly heard Grandmother's prayer asking that I get all the questions right and be given first-ranking as well. I don't care, though. In spite of that, I still believe in the Bodhisattva.

"We ask the Lord to open to her the gates of heaven. Let her return home where there is no death, only eternal happiness."
The Catholic father, officiating at the funeral in a purple cape,

stood at the dais of the chapel sometimes reciting scripture in a non-stop murmur, sometimes leading the gathered mourners in singing hymns.

When the congregation responded, uniting their voices in praise, it was like a muffled thunderclap.

Friends and relatives were scattered sparsely among the chapel's pews. Members of the older generation, in keeping with rural custom, stayed outside. It was proper that only younger people see one of their own generation laid to rest.[55] In addition, members of the older generation feared the strange Western religion that incorporated a devil spirit. They lingered downstairs below a covered arcade to wait for the ceremony to be over.

Except when the congregation suddenly sang loudly, awakening him, Li-li could not keep from drowsing. The solemn atmosphere of the Mass and the rain pattering on the roof conspired against his wakefulness. Finally, he dropped the hymnal he held in his hand; it fell heavily to the floor just as the priest intoned:

"Take this and eat, this is my body, sacrificed for you; take this and drink, this is my blood...."

Li-li didn't understand the meaning of the priest's words, but the idea of eating flesh and drinking blood made him a little sick.

"What's the matter with you, Li-li?" asked Third Uncle, seated next to him. He bent down and helped him retrieve the hymnal.

"My head is dizzy."

"It's stuffy in here. Let me take you outside for some air. This mid-summer heat is stifling."

During the night it had rained hard without pause; it was still raining in the morning. They slipped down the stairs from the second floor of the chapel into gusts of wind and rain.

"You really shouldn't have brought Li-li," said Li-li's aunt,[56] ducking into the first-floor arcade to escape the rain. "Bad spirits can frighten a small boy in this kind of place."

Third uncle shrugged his shoulders. "I know, but he wanted to come with me. He's already come twice and he certainly likes me to take him."

In the distance the sun had already set behind the bamboo grove on the river bank. Colorful evening clouds were fading and only a corner of dark, blue-green sky remained where the glowing light of Venus newly shone.

Relatives of all ages had moved wooden stools, chairs, and recliners into the drying court of the farmhouse. They gathered there outdoors to take advantage of the cool air, to talk, joke, and tell stories.

"Are you taking your nephew out to play?" Third Granduncle[57] asked.

"There's a funeral for the daughter-in-law of my wife's sister tomorrow," Third Uncle said. "I'm going to the funeral hall where the body will be placed during services. I want to see if I can help with preparations."

Third Uncle had one foot on a pedal and the other foot on the ground; Li-li, squeezed in between his arms, firmly grasped the middle of the handlebars with both hands and leaned out over the front wheel.

"Are you sure you want to go?" asked Third Uncle.

"Let me go take a look," Li-li said. "She was like my teacher. She came to our school one day and taught us."

"What do you mean she was a teacher one day?"

"She came and joined in."

"How do you know it's the same woman?" Third Uncle asked. "Are you sure? It seems like too much of a coincidence? Your recollection must be wrong."

"I don't know for sure, so I want to take a look."

"You can see only her photograph," Third Uncle explained. "She has already been placed in the coffin."

They left the rice-drying courtyard and, from out of the shade of a tree that blocked the sky, rode on a small narrow path into the light evening wind of the rice fields. In the luminous dusk, they followed a wider field path alongside a stream that flowed in the direction of the town. The church was on a dark corner of a crossroads. From faraway they could see its bright lights, but even with all the interior lighting, few people could be seen in the hall where the body lay.

The upper body of the deceased young woman had been prepared for viewing. Her face was pretty, though pale and slight. She wore a slight smile and faced the large room that was filled with yellow and white chrysanthemums, calligraphed mourning banners, and funeral scrolls with words of commiseration.

Two parishioners were making paper funeral flowers in the dim light of the adjacent office.

"Please," asked Third Uncle, "Can you tell me where the person in charge of the funeral has gone?"

"The deceased's husband went to buy some wire," a woman said. "The others went to eat. Who are you?"

"I'm...I'm her husband's cousin[58]."

"Oh...so you're a cousin of her husband. How sad," a second woman said. "She was three months pregnant and only twenty years old."

"The Lord Jesus will take them into heaven."

"Indeed, they can now return to our Heavenly Father's home."

While the two believers were expressing these religious sentiments, Li-li thought back on a particular morning. In the soft sunshine in the school yard, a group of students from the teaching college had showed up. They were attractive, exuberant, and friendly. They separated to go to different classes, but at noon each brought a few of Li-li's classmates to the mountain forest behind the school for an outing.

"Is this the teacher?" Third Uncle asked, gazing at the portrait in the funeral hall.

"It looks like her, but I don't remember for sure," Li-li said. "She told us many stories. She told us about a man who went to a temple. The merchants inside panicked and ran away. The man overturned the money tables, and he overturned the stools where pigeons were sold, saying he was the Son of God—like a prince, a really amazing man. If he touched a blind man, then the blind man could see. If he touched a cripple, then the cripple could get up and walk. The man did a number of these things.

"One morning when he was hungry, he saw a fig tree beside the road, but he couldn't find anything on it but leaves. So he cast a spell: `You will never again bear fruit.' The fig tree immediately withered and died. I only remember this much, and I don't remember why he wanted to put a curse on the tree."

112

"Uh?" Third Uncle said. "It's just a story."

Li-li also thought about the time they had sat in the shade of the woods. The teacher stood on the grass in the sunlight, the blue sky and mountain stream behind her. She spoke with confidence and composure, telling religious stories. As she spoke, beads of sweat formed on her face, and she wore a slight smile. In the forest there was only stillness and the sound of the mountain stream.

"Oh, I remember another story," Li-li said. "There were seven brothers and then the oldest died. But because his wife had no children, the second oldest married the widow so that his older brother would have an heir. But the second brother had no children either, and he died. The third brother, fourth brother, right down to the seventh, all did the same. Finally, the woman died, too."

"We don't have such kinds of marriage," Third Uncle said.

"I know," Li-li said. "And the story has a problem because these kinds of people aren't supposed to really die; they're supposed to return to life. Okay. But when they come back to life, whose wife of the seven is she? They all had married her."

"Ha! You ask a tough question."

"The answer is that she didn't become anyone's wife again," Li-li said, "because she became an angel in heaven."

"Oh, so that's it," Third Uncle said.

"Yesterday evening we should have put up a tarp," someone cried out. "I saw that halo around the moon; and even though the clouds were moving fast, the barometer was very low."

"Everybody wants to blame Uncles[59] Ah Shen and Wen Chi, the two brothers, for last night," another man said. "Everyone said it would be best to have food at the funeral supper but no alcohol. The brothers said if someone drinks one or two bottles of Red Dew rice wine to slake their thirst, what's the harm in that? So then everyone decided the brothers were right and felt free to drink. Everyone rationalized that to have had so many good dishes with nothing to drink would really have been unfortunate. That was all right, but then what happened? Everyone got drunk! My god! What idiots! It was a funeral supper intended to help bring some solace to the mourners; it wasn't

113

supposed to be a wild party! As far as I'm concerned such people can go to Hell, just as their Jesus Christ church says."

Another person said, "Such a hard rain. The guests who are crowded into the pavilion below are becoming restless. If we'd raised a rain tarp in the big garden grounds, everyone would be much more comfortable."

"It's all the same," one person said. "Just wait a while, the rain coming from the mountains will be so hard that a tarp or umbrellas will be of no use anyway. Sooner or later everything is going to get drenched."

"It's Heaven's way of showing pity, dropping so much rain," a grieving young woman said. "Brother Ah Hsiang was very kind toward his wife, but his mother was hostile to the daughter-in-law. The young woman was only a student at the teacher's college, but she had to teach, do the laundry, and cook, and she married into a big family. For her to marry into our kind of farm-village family wasn't easy."

"Why's that?" a young man asked playfully and laughed. "Farmers can handle their chores in the fields in the daytime and in bed in the evening."

"You won't get any tears at your death. To speak such words in this kind of place...."

"Even though I have already suffered so much, I still embrace the faith.

"The fig tree's return to life can be seen as a metaphor. Several times its branches put forth tender shoots. When the leaves appear, you know summer is not far off.

"Our bodies come from the clay of the earth and return to the clay; let her body return to the original source as well; let her soul find peace on the last day, the resurrection."

It was chaotic outside the church where many flower-decorated cars along the roadside were beginning to move into traffic. Honor guard and band members were continuing to gather on the side of the road by the arcade, forming rows like a military deployment. The people who had been waiting for the procession to begin and had grown tired came to life and suddenly began opening their umbrellas and putting on their raincoats. They walked in droves into the pouring rain.

114

On the surface of the road, the rain water was high enough to form small waves. Water flowed loudly in the ditches. In the distance a church officer, wearing a faded red ceremonial cape, led the procession. He looked up at the sky and blew on a long, thin copper horn. At the sad liquid cry of the instrument, the rank and file of the funeral procession began officially to move.

*"This kind of Chinese-Western funeral ceremony is very strange,"
Auntie said.*

"Yes," Third Uncle said. "In the Catholic parish, everyone's singing one moment, then in the next moment everyone's reading Buddhist sutras. The congregation stands up for a while, then it sits down for a while. It's hard for the people of our village to know how to act, especially if the villager is illiterate."

"Do you also want to go with me up the mountain, Li-li? It's a hard climb," Auntie said, firmly embracing his shoulders. "Perhaps you never actually saw this cousin's wife."

"I saw her one time last year during winter vacation. Mother and I attended her wedding ceremony...."

The band was playing the funeral song, and the music brought tears to Li-li's eyes. He cried and bit his lip.

"Perhaps she really was their teacher," Third Uncle said. "She spent one day teaching them."

"All right, you can lean on your Auntie a little. You're already soaked through," she said. "I don't want the rain to wash you away."

78

The Main Point

The newspaper says a primary school in Japan this year has begun teaching students to write movie scripts as part of an effort to improve writing education. They think this composition method will help cultivate a student's objectivity.

A girl in the school's second grade wrote a play called *Year's End.* A famous movie playwright explained that the entire piece boiled down to these several scenes:

1.   In the street in front of a temple, many large flags have been positioned announcing year-end sales. (Camera shoots from a distance.)
2.   A fluttering pennant—red, yellow, and green—is raised above the others. (Camera gradually makes it the center of the scene.)
3.   A toy store displays a huge quantity of rubber mice. (Camera pays special attention to this.)
4.   Kids call out to their mothers, wanting to buy clothing. (The behavior of the people is shown on camera.)
5.   On the road, crowds of people carry many parcels from the store. (Return to location of the first distant shot of the scene.)

These things I seem to understand, but don't. But if I say "walking happily," I know it's better to write "hand in hand, skipping away." I understand this. Mother says whether one writes scripts or not, or understands them or not, doesn't matter. The main point is to see a thing and not let your attention waver even a little, to try to see its very essence.

79

Swan Lake

In music class today, our teacher introduced us to the ancient wind instrument, the long flute, then she played a long-flute concert, *Swan Lake,* on the electric phonograph. It was really beautiful, soft, and mysterious.

80

Flag Fluttering

Philippine President Garcia has come to our country for a six-day visit. His entourage includes five cabinet ministers and three national assemblymen. They came for a conference on Asia's struggle against Communism. President Chiang and Vice President Chen went to the airport to welcome them. Bands performed the two national anthems. The Navy gave them a twenty-one-gun salute.

I asked Mother if firing so many guns was to express that our country is stronger than theirs. Mother said that if our president goes to another country on a visit, the people there also will give a twenty-one-gun salute. It expresses the utmost respect of one nation for another and is the strongest and warmest welcome.

When these distinguished guests entered Taipei, more than one hundred thousand people and students along the streets waved the flags of both nations.

Today after school a big fog blew in. It happened that we held our flag-lowering ceremony just at the time when the fog was thickest. We could see the flag fluttering above the fog in the pure sky; it was a joyful moment. But when we lowered the flag into the heavy fog, the occasion turned very solemn.

81

Pearl Tears

Lin Yu-ts'ai, the miner's son, has once again been caught stealing. This time he took Wang Hsiao-ming's Eight Immortals[60] knife. Because of Wang Hsiao-ming's bringing her knife to class, the teacher hit her five hard strokes on the palm. Lin Yu-ts'ai got ten strokes and had to stand out in the hall. The teacher was so angry that she said she wanted to have Lin Yu-ts'ai expelled from school.

Both Wu Chih-kuo's father and Wang Hsiao-ming's father are customs employees. Wu Chih-kuo says Wang Hsiao-ming's father often takes things that belong to Customs, either confiscated or received as a gift from private parties. In truth, this and stealing are not so different. When Wang Hsiao-ming heard this, he was very angry. He said Wu Chih-kuo's father can be blamed for the same thing. Their family often has imported apples to eat.

There are students who especially pity Lin Yu-ts'ai. Several months ago a rock in a mine tunnel fell on his father, crushing one leg. Now he depends on relief money to live. Everyone signed a sheet of note paper and wrote a sentence wishing him well.

The class leader, representing all of us, took the paper and gave it to Lin Yu-ts'ai. He immediately broke down and cried. Because his punishment was to stand in the hallway, he did not dare leave his place; and because it was after class, many students from other classes gathered around to look. The principal just then arrived and saw what was happening. She went over to investigate.

When he saw the principal, Lin Yu-ts'ai was so startled his whole body began to tremble, and, rather surprisingly, he stopped crying. The principal asked him what was going on, but he dared not to answer.

"He stole something and our teacher punished him with standing detention," the class leader said. "But it's sad because his family is poor, and so he often steals things. Our teacher wants to expel him."

I don't know why, but the principal also began to cry. Her eyes first moistened and then shed pearl tears. A moment later she suddenly embraced Lin Yu-ts'ai, who also began to cry. Seeing the principal crying, we students all cried, too.

"I'll go speak with your teacher and ask for leniency," the principal said. "But you certainly don't want to make this mistake again."

82

Plum Monsoon

On account of a bad cold, I almost couldn't get out of bed today. Yesterday around dusk I began to feel dizzy and my nose began to run. Recently the weather has been unsettled, changing from clear skies to clouds, to rain and then to thunder. The humidity is high and the wind blows on our sticky sweat. Many people at school have caught colds, and I finally caught mine.

Mother says I shouldn't read the newspaper in detail because it takes too much time. I should only read in the paper what she first checks in red. During the Plum Monsoon, I must practice the piano and painting in earnest, so that when summer comes I can seriously train my body and get in better shape. She also doesn't want me to write in my journal every day. In truth, there's already no way I can hear or think about so many new things. I need to grow some more and deepen my learning; then I'll be better able to understand what is most significant in the world around me.

83

Crime and Transportation

Taipei City Public Health Clinic statistics show that last year in Taipei City the five greatest causes of death were (in order of greatest frequency): cerebral hemorrhage (stroke); heart disease; accidental violence; pneumonia; and cancer-related illnesses and other tumors.

Seven years ago the main causes of death were stroke; diarrhea, intestinal, or bowel catarrh; indigestion, dyspepsia, and other illnesses of the digestive system; tuberculosis; heart disease; and pneumonia.

The changes in the list reflect the improvement in both medical treatment and facilities, according to the newspaper. Diarrhea and catarrh, for example, have ceased to be a common cause of death. But following the social improvements, suicides, murders and car accidents, etc.—in other words, crime and transportation problems—have increased shockingly.

For the whole province last year, the population was 10.53 million;[61] Taipei City had 870,000. This year, in just the first four months, Taipei added thirty thousand persons.

84

War Clouds

War clouds are gathering on Kinmen's front lines.
America has given our military a shipment of new high-speed

war planes, the F-104. The F-104 is supposed to be better than the F-86. Is it? Not long ago, an F-86 fighter jet crashed on a mission in the south. In the course of its crash, it struck forty homes, killing ten persons and injuring fifteen.

America also gave our country a super-fast naval transport.

That country seems to often aid our country, as at Kinmen where it constructed underground caves and bomb shelters, and at Keelung, where it built a Navy dormitory.

85

Spy Plane

The Soviet Union has succeeded in launching a four-and-a-half ton satellite spaceship. This manned craft is the heaviest body to go into space orbit. Not too long before, the Soviet Union knocked down an American spy plane within its air space with a new kind of air-to-air missile.

86

Engine Displacement

Until now, our nation had never produced its own small car. Yue Loong Company is the successful manufacturer. The car can travel sixty kilometers in one hour. Every day one new car can be built. After one month, the production level will rise to six vehicles per day. The engine has forty-two horsepower. The engine displacement is 1200 cc. To promote local parts makers, the car will use parts manufactured in Taiwan. The Presidential Office has taken the lead in placing an order for one car. Yue Loong also produces a basic diesel public bus, which now is being introduced to Taipei City's transportation system.

I remember that the Taiwan Railway Administration recently was using new diesel electric steam engines, but these were imported from abroad. The engine is the kind that's not supposed to lose power when climbing a steep slope.

87

Gym Class

Today in gym class we played dodgeball. The bigger, stronger students are able to dodge quickly and use their arm strength to maintain the advantage. The others usually all get quickly knocked out of the game. Every day for the last couple of weeks I have been using the horizontal bar and practicing the long jump. I believe I'm on the way to having a stronger and healthier body.

88

Sea Eel

Father said he really wanted to spend the weekend with Mother and me, but he still wanted to go fishing. The result was we accompanied him fishing.

We went to the seaside before evening to a stretch of beach where the rocks at the foot of the mountain extend into the sea. Father prepared his fishing tackle and cast his bait into the surf. We then had a picnic.

It soon became dark. But just before it did, the planet Venus floated on the horizon and brightened. Then in the night sky shining stars began to appear, including constellations. We sat on the large rocks of the shore and talked.

Sometimes I felt bored on the trip, so I used my lamp to explore along the edge of the sea and among the large rocks with cracks and holes hollowed by the action of waves.

I saw a sea eel as thick as my arm crawling on a reef and looking at the moon.

89

Mountain Sheep

Several classmates agreed that today during the noon rest period we would go to the back side of the mountain to gather bayberries.[62] We climbed a tree and could see on the far side of the forest a patch of grass where ten mountain sheep were each tied to wooden stakes.

We at once climbed down the tree, left the bayberries, and ran to try to get the sheep to play. Some classmates attempted to ride on their backs; others grabbed their horns and wrestled them. I fed them some grass.

90

Once a Sick Person Starts to Run, I Can't Catch Up

Today playing blindman's buff, I suddenly bumped into Hu Ling-yu. She used her handkerchief to help wipe sweat from my face, and then she said she wanted to kiss my lips. I said she could kiss my forehead, face, and nose, but not my lips. That could make her pregnant. She laughed at me as if I were a fool. She said kissing for just a moment doesn't matter; it's when you kiss for a long time that you can get pregnant. How true this is, I can't say, but I didn't let her kiss my lips.

A dog came to the trees around the yard. Its face, neck, hindquarters, and tail still had some white fur, but the rest of its body was mangy. It had bare patches with either pink open sores or dry brown skin. The two rows of teats were shriveled and sunken.

Li-li sat reading at the top of the stone stairs in the shade of the trees. He had no idea where the dog had come from or when it had first appeared. It stood now hesitating on the road at the foot of the stairs. Surprised by a look from Li-li, it immediately took flight, disappearing into the underbrush of the woods. Li-li wasn't absolutely certain he had really seen the strange dog. Perhaps, owing to his absorption in his reading, he had only imagined it. He collected his books and went to investigate, quietly stepping down the stone stairs flanked by the old trees on either side.

"What are you doing?" his mother asked.

"A strange dog ran into the grove of trees."

"Stay far away from it. It could bite you."

"It's a timid dog," Li-li said.

The dog had its head buried in a den in the grove of trees; only its hindquarters were visible through the leaves and branches.

"I can't see any dog. What dog?" the mother said.

"It's like a dog with scabies skin."

"Oh," the mother said. "We should leave here at once."

Later, Li-li's father had a different view regarding the mangy dog. "It only needs some food to eat; later its skin will get better. Also give it some salad oil with its food; salad oil can help cure skin diseases."

"Once it could have been a beautiful dog," Li-li said.

"What are you thinking?" the father said.

Li-li blushed.

"Is it a male or female?"

"It has teats," Li-li said, gesticulating.

His father scowled and said, "It's a female."

The father did not say more. After lunch, Li-li took some leftovers, filled up a big bowl, and added several spoonfuls of salad oil.

During the entire afternoon, the bowl of food went untouched. There was also no sign of the dog in the grove of trees in the corner of the yard.

By evening the food was spoiled. By the second day, the sun had baked it dry. Li-li started off again to look for the dog.

"The same kind of mangy dog," Mrs. Wang, a neighbor said, "was hiding last year in the Chang family's back yard. They couldn't drive it away and later it gave birth to some pups. They never saw her again."

"Every day the garbage on the other side of the river is overturned," another neighbor said. "Several times I've seen the dog near the overturned garbage."

Li-li found the garbage site, but he didn't find the dog where the garbage had been knocked over. Perhaps the dog had already rifled through the garbage and right now was drinking at the river. This one small section of the riverbank occupied by garbage piles was also overgrown with the spreading vines and luxuriant, glossy leaves of morning glories, all entwined like a blanket of purple flowers. The dog was standing on a sandbar drinking water.

"Hi, little dog," Li-li shouted. "Here's a piece of cookie to eat, and he threw it in the dog's direction.

It startled her, and she straightened up and ran.

"Hey," the neighbor boy accompanying Li-li scolded. "You're a dumb dog."

They ran across the cement bridge, leaped up a flight of stone steps, and followed the river bank and the small road that passed by project houses. They chased after the dog to the upper reaches of the stream, but ended finding only a school of small fish in a pool, and dragonflies, thick above lush water grasses.

"It really is a dumb dog," the neighbor boy said.

When Li-li entered the medical clinic, his plump uncle, the doctor, was seated on a sofa reading a book.

"Oh, it's my precious nephew," he said "Are you sick?"

"There's a dog that's sick."

"Oh? And did you bring it with you?" asked the doctor. "Where is it?"

"I can't catch it."

"Come again? Are you playing a little joke on me? If so, it's a good one. I'm bored. It's the right time to play one on me."

"What I'm saying is I saw a dog with mange. Can you heal it?"

"A dog with favus, you mean; that's a skin disease," said the doctor with a touch of pride, nodding his head. "It must be fed some pellagra preventative."

"What is pellagra preventative, Fatty Uncle?"

"A kind of vitamin we get from the tobacco leaf," the doctor said. "Where is this poor creature?"

"I can't catch it."

"Are you saying it's a wild dog?"

"Yes. But it's a timid wild dog."

"It's still dangerous. You must have your father think out a safe way to catch it. He's a very smart man," the doctor said. "I've never once left my clinic to catch a sick man. I'm too fat. Once a sick person starts to run, I can't catch up, ha, ha." Holding up his index finger as a sign that he was engaged in remembering, he said, "I'll give this matter some thought. As I recall, didn't we rescue a turkey last year?"

"That's right. You are a good-hearted doctor, Fatty Uncle."

Li-li and his father gave serious thought to how to catch the dog, including the idea of making a cage trap with a spring door on a netted box; using a long bamboo pole with a round net at the end; or using a bow and arrow with the bamboo arrow tipped in anesthetic. But these were only ideas on paper. Furthermore, no one knew where the dog now was.

Then one evening, the doctor and Li-li's father were returning along the road from fishing when they met the dog. Under a street lamp in the yellow dusk, the dog was being ridden by a large male dog. Several other young male dogs were barking and milling around.

"My god," the father said. "This is the little female dog that Li-li saw."

"It appears rabid. See, when it is indulging in that kind of plea-sure," the doctor said, "it can be crushed to death, crushed to death."

"What a tragedy."

"It's a dog," the doctor said, and mumbled again to himself, "It's a dog."

"I don't see how we can help," the father said. "It'll get preg-nant, its skin will rot, and then it will finally die in some god-for-saken place."

"I wish I could shoot it."

"It's a tragic life."

"It's a dog," the doctor said.

Li-li had almost forgotten about the dog. He hadn't seen it since the day on the river bank. One day, however, waking from a noon nap and getting ready to go out to play, he was surprised to spot it lying sick on the stone stairs in the shade of the trees.

Hesitating a moment and looking into the trees, Li-li cried "Mama! The dog has come back. Come quick! Quick! Bring something to give it to eat."

Several days later, Li-li's father wearing gloves, led the dog by a chain around its neck into the doctor's office. The doctor gave it an injection and every meal thereafter put several powder medicines into its food.

"It will recover won't it?" Li-li asked. "It will, won't it, Fatty Uncle?"

"It will fatten up," the doctor said and laughed. "Just like me, just the same."

91

Shark Skins

The Provincial Fisheries Agency is promoting the use and tanning of the entire skin of sharks as a line of export to secure foreign exchange. The following rules now govern work procedures of local fish markets in this regard:

When cleaning the fish, cut the head portion to remove viscera. Do not injure or destroy the abdomen. Workers who violate this will be fired. Bosses will have their licenses revoked.

I don't understand how you can remove the entrails of a big fish without cutting open the belly. And how can you move such a big fish without using hand hooks?

92

The Grain Bureau

The provincial governor is concerned about the rising price of rice. It was recently reported to him that imported rice from Thailand is not suitable for human consumption. He asked the chairman of the Grain Bureau if exports of Taiwan-grown rice can be reduced a little. Selling local rice and buying imported rice didn't seem like a good idea.

The Grain Bureau chairman responded that a ton of our rice

distributed abroad brings US$144. When we buy Thailand rice, each ton costs only US$101. By this rice-substitution practice, the nation earns US$34 American dollars in foreign exchange on every ton.

Upon hearing this, the provincial governor laughed and said, "This sounds good, but you can't imagine how many letters I get complaining about this practice."

93

"Oh My Big!"

The newspaper reports that life now is not so easy for lower-level military and government personnel, nor for staff persons of public schools. Special government officials and legislators in the central government, by contrast, are making out fine. To narrow the income gap, government personnel in the military establishment and staff persons of public schools will now receive a pay adjustment.

But one government employee is very angry. He sent a letter to the newspaper saying that to adjust salaries would lead to price inflation. Already one *chin*[63] of pork sells for NT$20. Previously, he could buy pork once a month; now he can't buy it at all.

The government employee wrote, "If one *chin* of pork were to sell at less than NT$20...oh my big!" Here I'm certain the newspaper made a typographic error, and printed "Oh my big!" for "Oh my god!"[64]

94

Tidal Wave

A big earthquake in Chile triggered a tsunami tidal wave in the Pacific Ocean. In Japan the tsunami lifted fishing boats into the streets. In Hawaii waves swept over sandy beaches and poured into streets, wrecking homes and office buildings. Australia and the

Philippines also suffered disasters.

This was a really terrifying tsunami, with waves of ten meters. In Japan it killed one hundred fifty-five people in one fishing village alone.

In Keelung a bridge was washed out. Among the people who escaped in a panic to higher ground, some managed to return to schools and take the boys and girls home.

Twenty minutes after the Chilean earthquake occurred, it was detected on instruments here. The radio said that the Pacific Ocean's average depth is 4,300 meters. A tidal wave would travel at a speed of seven hundred kilometers per hour crossing it. The distance from Chile to Taiwan is 20,000 kilometers. The tidal wave would, therefore, strike Taiwan in not less than thirty-two hours. Accordingly, the tsunami reached the province at 11:00 a.m. yesterday.

The last time Taiwan experienced a tidal wave was eighty-three years ago. It was also caused by a big earthquake. The waves in Keelung at that time suddenly flowed toward the outer sea, exposing some of the sea bottom. Moments later, a great wall of water from beyond the harbor came crashing toward the inner harbor and into downtown Keelung, as well as into the towns of Tamsui, Chilungtou, and Chinpaoli, destroying countless seashore residences and drowning one hundred people.

95

Destitute Status

I asked Mother who is K'ang Yu-wei. She said that he was a very famous scholar and politician in the last years of the Ch'ing Dynasty. Once he helped Emperor Kuang Hsu[65], who wanted to overthrow the Empress Dowager Tzu Hsi and rebuild the declining nation.

The newspaper says Mr. K'ang Yu-wei's wife is living in dire straits in Taipei. She has no money and is in poor health.

Mr. K'ang Yu-wei has been dead more than thirty years. His son lives with his wife in Taipei. He's employed by the Railway

Bureau as an engineer, but suffers constantly from asthma. A grandchild is an electrical machinist, but in order to look after both his father and grandmother, he must stay with them in the same hospital room.[66] He has had to quit his job more than once.

K'ang Yu-wei's wife has requested "destitute status" from the city government in order to receive cancer treatment at the Railway Bureau Hospital.

The K'ang family originally had wealth and power. It's hard to understand how conditions of human life can change from honor to dishonor so suddenly.

96

Dr. Zhivago

Because Father doesn't read the newspaper in detail, sometimes the family newspaper never gets opened. Therefore, I gave him a phone call to tell him the news I just read. Not long ago, he read a novel called *Doctor Zhivago* by a Russian novelist. According to today's paper, the novelist just died from an illness.

As I expected, Father expressed surprise. He wanted me to wait a moment while he got the book. Then he said he would read me a part of a poem from the author's novel:

> The loud applause is over. Here on the stage,
> I lean against a pillar, listening
> for some echo from afar,
> for a cue of coming events.
> . . . .
> Living life to the very end isn't a child's game.[67]

Both China

In recent months, Tibetan guerrillas and the Chinese Communist Red Army have been fighting a bitter war. Casualties are heavy, with one battle alone claiming the lives of 2,400 guerrillas. Tibetan guerrillas have downed four Communist bombers.

I asked Mother why Tibet and Communist China were fighting. Mother said Tibet and Communist China are both China, that it's a civil war.

I asked Mother if China isn't really made up of several countries. She answered no, that it's only one.

98

Mr. Eisenhower

Today the American president, Mr. Eisenhower, came to visit our country. The Chinese Communists protested his visit and, in a savage artillery barrage, fired more than 30,000 shells toward Kinmen.

Compared to the time when the Philippine president came here, this visit was much more important. The grounds for the welcoming ceremony were grander, and five hundred thousand people assembled outside the Presidential Office. Twenty-five bands played welcome music and ten thousand colored balloons were released into the air as fireworks exploded.

This time the gun salute was also different.

Mr. Eisenhower was aboard an American war vessel entering Keelung Harbor. Our country's fleet of warships sailed to the outer sea to welcome him. The American president's flagship entered Keelung Harbor's breakwater, then fired a twenty-one-gun salute in respect. Our country then gave the American warship a twenty-one-gun salute in the direction of America in respect.

No Manners

The doctor in the medical services room, accompanied by our teacher, came to our classroom to find a student. He wanted to find the one who has recently been using a rubber-band slingshot with rocks to hit students during class time.

Our teacher hoped the student would come forward and confess, but no one did.

Mother says the doctor was being paid back by whoever the resentful student was. She says the doctor is a snob. He often has little patience with students of poor families. One time he asked a student to look at something. The student didn't say anything, so the doctor pushed him out of his chair.

Then he scolded the boy for having no manners and no upbringing and even for making a face at him. The truth, however, is that the student had a painful eye problem and was blinking and blinking.

100

Farewell, Farewell

The school term has ten days left, but the ceremony for the graduating class was held before school ends.

Each graduating student, in high spirits, had a new haircut and pressed clothes. I saw several pairs of leather shoes all carefully polished and shined. Old freshly washed cloth shoes were also spiffed up with white powder. One tall boy, though, still had no shoes, but he did cut his toenails.

The mothers of the graduating students got dressed in their best clothes, and the teachers received them enthusiastically. All the mothers smiled.

The graduation ceremony was held in the auditorium, and our fourth and fifth grades were invited to watch. A number of electric fans revolved from the ceiling. The doors and windows also were opened as wide as possible. Even so, the auditorium was still way too hot and humid. Outside, the air was filled with the rising and falling chorus of cicadas.

Many of the distinguished guests spoke a long time about the pursuit of this goal or that. Then, finally, the diplomas were handed out.

The son of a factory worker was the speaker for the graduating class. During the earlier speech competition, he had been very dignified and composed. This time he stumbled over his words and, crying like a girl, couldn't finish. I really couldn't understand what he was saying near the end.

When it came time for the farewell song to be sung, two graduates rose. Both belong to a choir group that won the All-City Choir Competition. Their singing rose and fell smoothly, but not long after starting, one of them also began to cry. Then the other began to cry as well. Finally, only the music of the piano kept on.

What they sang was this:

> The school's trees are green, and the grass is lush.
> Fresh rain to them is a precious oil.
> Together we study every day—what happiness!
> So how can we bear to part on this morning?
>
> There are many forks in the roads of the world.
> And many are those who sail this morning.
>
> But listening to the singing of the farewell song,
> It's sad to think of leaving old friends.
>
> When will we meet again in this world?

Unexpectedly, the principal also cried openly. Then the ceremony promptly concluded. She bade the graduates farewell and said that, despite the great difficulties of present times, we are all still optimistic and hopeful.

"One day," she said, "you will think back to your childhood

years and will realize that they were the happiest time of your life."
She began to cry again. "Farewell, my beloved children." Then she
waved good-bye with one hand and with the other brushed away
tears with a handkerchief. "Farewell, farewell."

The End

Notes on the translation

1. One of several common names for *Miscanthus sinesis*, a grass with long serrated leaves and tall plumes in fall. The Chinese name is *mang ts'ao*.

2. Schools in Taiwan hold classes on Saturday until noon. Government offices are open until noon on Saturday as well.

3. All provinces of China are represented in Taiwan's citizenry (just as are all the major Chinese cuisines). One reason for this is that some 1.5 million Chinese, including 600,000 soldiers, came to Taiwan in 1949 after the mainland fell to the Communists.

4. The hot pepper sauce is *la-chiao chiang*, used commonly in Szechwan and Hunan cuisine.

5. Keelung Harbor and Keelung City are located in northeast Taiwan roughly seventeen miles northeast of Taipei on the Pacific Ocean. Today Keelung is a major port for containerized shipping.

6. Yehliu, which means "wild willow," is located not far north of Keelung. Where this rock promontory extends farthest into the sea, it is called, according to its likeness, Turtle Island.

7. The *Kuo-yu re-pau* is a newspaper published in Taipei for children and others learning Mandarin Chinese. All written characters in the newspaper are printed with their phonetic symbols.

8. Matsu, of the famous island pair Quemoy (Kinmen) and Matsu, lies in the Taiwan Strait just off the mainland China coast. The islands are the territory of the Republic of China on Taiwan and were defended successfully at a great cost of life against repeated attacks by Communist China beginning in 1949.

9. Sun Moon Lake, located in the mountains of central Taiwan, was formed by construction of a large electricity-generating dam. The

lake is one of Taiwan's major scenic attractions.

10. Hsien Tung Yen, or "Fairy Cave," is a cliff cave and tourist attraction located on the northwest shore of the entrance to Keelung Harbor.

11. The character *hsi* means "happiness," hence two such characters together mean "double happiness."

12. *Chiu-chiu* is the Chinese for "maternal uncle" ("mother's brother").

13. *Piao-hsiung ti* is the Chinese for "male first-cousin."

14. *I-piao ke* is a "cousin on the mother's side."

15. *Lao-hu*, or "tiger." The mispronunciation, *lao-ku*, is gibberish.

16. A "godown" is a warehouse or storage facility.

17. *Euphoria longana* is a tree that bears a pulpy, edible fruit said to resemble "dragon eyes."

18. Traditionally a space was left before the name of the president of the Republic of China when the president was mentioned in certain printed publications. A conventional sign of respect, it occurs thus in the Chinese text of Li-li's journal.

19. Chiang Kai-shek, or Chiang Chung-cheng, the first-through-fifth president of the Republic of China.

20. "Kiss" is written in English in the Chinese text of Li-li's journal.

21. The island of Kinmen is also known in the West as Quemoy.

22. Taiwan's second largest city and largest port, situated on the southwest coast of the island.

23. Hengch'un is a town located in the extreme south of Taiwan.

24. *Ku-ma* is the word used here for an "aunt on the father's side."

25. Located in the northeast county of Ilan and down the Pacific coast from Keelung.

26. Called *t'ien-keng*, literally "field ditches."

27. *Wai-p'o* is the word used here for "maternal grandmother."

28. "Little Uncle" (*Hsiao chiou-chiou* or "youngest maternal uncle") is also referred to as "Uncle Man" in the Chinese text. For ease of identification, I have used "Little Uncle" throughout.

29. *Wai-sheng* is the word used here for "nephew," or "child of one's sister."

30. Five New Taiwan dollars, or five *k'uai*. The exchange rate in early 1998 was approximately thirty-three New Taiwan dollars to one U.S. dollar. At the time in which this story is set, 1960, the exchange rate was roughly US$1=NT$40.

31. The common name for *Syzigium samarangense* of the myrtle family. The wax apple produces a highly edible pink fruit whose shape resembles a bell and is about the size of medium-sized pair.

32. Traditionally, the Civil Service Examination is the meritocratic door to government employment for intellectuals and scholars.

33. A game of tag.

34. A *chia* = 0.97 hectare; a hectare = 2.47 acres.

35. This was a governmental body that held the authority to elect the president and the vice president. In 1996, this function was given to the voters through direct elections.

36. A night market in Keelung. *Miao K'o* literally means "temple entrance."

37. This "uncle" in Chinese is *shu-shu*, indicating a younger brother of one's father.

38. *Shui-chiau,* or "boiled dumplings."

39. One of the main characters in the famous Chinese story, *Journey to the West*.

40. *Ta-lung* literally means "big dragon."

41. *Turdus poliocephalus*, a singing bird of the thrush family.

42. This day falls on the 28th of March and is also known as Youth Day.

43. Sun Yat-sen, or Sun Chungshan, is the founding father of the Republic of China.

44. Formulated in the early twenties by Dr. Sun Yat-sen, the Three Principles of the People (*San min chu i*) are customarily summed up as Nationalism, Democracy, and Livelihood.

45. *Chiou-ma,* or "maternal aunt (mother's brother's wife)."

46. A holiday when families return to the graves of their ancestors in the countryside to worship and to clean grave sites. It is observed on April 5th (on April 4th during leap years).

47. The Chinese female incarnation of *Avalokitesvara Bodhisattva* known as the Goddess of Mercy. In Taiwan, this deity enjoys enormous popularity among the island's large Buddhist community.

48. In Mandarin Chinese, the equivalent of "ABC" is *po p'o mo fo*, the first four symbols of the National Phonetic Symbols (*Kuo-yu chu-yin fu-hao*).

49. Taiwan's largest and most influential research organization (now under the Office of the President).

50. The "noon rest" or *hsiu-hsi*, is not just a custom of schoolchildren in Taiwan (and China), but an institution among most of the adult work force as well.

51. The Kuomintang. This is the ruling political party in the Republic of China. It was founded by Dr. Sun Yat-sen and is also known as the Nationalist Party.

52. A term for a variety of foods that are characterized by a meat wrapped inside a salty or spicy cooked "pancake" or tortilla-like wrapper.

53. "Uncle" here is *po-po* in Chinese. Though its primary meaning is "father's elder brother," it is often used, as in this instance, as a courtesy address for a familiar friend of the senior generation.

54. The rainy season in northern Taiwan is also known as the Plum Rains or Plum Monsoon. From April to June, spring winds bring a warm steady drizzle to the island. The typhoon season (roughly June through September) usually begins soon after, or slightly overlaps, the Plum Rains.

55. Literally, "White hair does not see off black hair."

56. *I-ma*, or "the married sister of one's mother." This is Third Uncle's sister.

57. *Shu kung*, or a "father's uncle."

58. *Piao-hsiung ti*, or "first cousins on the maternal side."

59. *Shu*, or a "younger brother of one's father."

60. *Pa hsien*, a special group of Taoists whose members are said to

have attained immortality. One of the most popularly represented subjects in China, the Eight Immortals are associated with happiness.

61. Taiwan's population today (1998) is more than twenty-two million.

62. A Chinese pound, one *catty*, or 1.33 lb.

63. Chinese bayberry, or *Myrica rubra*; a small tree with small, reddish, edible fruit.

64. The Chinese character *t'ien*, or "heaven (god)," has two horizontal strokes rather than one, but is otherwise identical to the character *ta*, or "big."

65. The reigning title of Emperor Teh Tsung, who was on the throne from 1875 to 1908.

66. In Taiwan there usually are no regular visiting hours in hospitals as in the United States. Visitors generally can come and go any time to see patients. It is also common for at least one family member to be posted in the hospital room of a relative at all times.

67. The poem is "Hamlet," from the pen of Yurii Andreievich Zhivago, the fictional hero of Boris Pasternak's novel.

TUNG NIEN (the pen name of Ch'en Shun-hsin) was born in the rainy Pacific port of Keelung, Taiwan, where his novel *Setting Out (Ch'u-lu)* (1993) is set. Before becoming a published writer, he worked as a marine radio operator. In 1978, he participated in the international Writing Program at University of Iowa. He is the author of three volumes of short stories and four novels, including the prize-winning novel *The Bodhisattva of Pen Yuan Temple* (1994), whose protagonist is the young hero of *Setting Out,* now grown up; and the novella *Last Winter* (1983), which has been made into a film. Tung Nien is, at present, assistant general manager of Lien-ching Book Company, one of Taiwan's major literary publishers. He lives in Taipei with his wife and children.

MIKE O'CONNOR was born in the rainy Pacific port of Aberdeen, Washington, and grew up on the Olympic Peninsula. After more than a decade engaged in farming and woods-related work, he spent twelve years as a journalist and student of Chinese culture in Taiwan. His books of original poems and translations include *The Basin: Life in a Chinese Province* and *The Rainshadow,* both from Empty Bowl (Port Townsend); *When I Find You Again, It Will Be in Mountains* and *Colors of Daybreak and Dusk,* selected poems of Chia Tao (779-843), both from Tangram (Berkeley). His work *Only a Friend Can Know*—poems and translations on the Chinese theme of *chih-yin*—can be found in the on-line poetry journal *Mudlark* at www.unf.edu/mudlark.

Pleasure Boat Studio Books

William Slaughter, *The Politics of My Heart*
(ISBN 0-9651413-0-6)

Frances Driscoll, *The Rape Poems*
(ISBN 0-9651413-1-4)

Michael Blumenthal, *When History Enters the House:
 Essays from Central Europe*
(ISBN 0-9651413-2-2)

Tung Nien, *Setting Out: The Education of Li-li,*
in English Translation by Mike O'Connor
(ISBN 0-9651413-3-0)

Irving Warner, *In Solitude's Eye: Short Stories*
(ISBN 0-9651413-4-9)
Forthcoming

From *Pleasure Boat Studio,*

an essay written by Ouyang Xiu,
Song Dynasty poet, essayist, and scholar,
on the twelfth day of the twelfth month
in the *renwu* year (January 25, 1043)

*I have heard of men of antiquity who fled from the world
to distant rivers and lakes and refused to their dying day
to return. They must have found some source of pleasure
there. If one is not anxious for profit, even at the risk of
danger, or is not convicted of a crime and forced to em-
bark; rather, if one has a favorable breeze and gentle seas
and is able to rest comfortably on a pillow and mat, sailing several hundred miles in a single day, then is boat
travel not enjoyable? Of course, I have no time for such
diversions. But since 'pleasure boat' is the designation of
boats used for such pastimes, I have now adopted it as the
name of my studio. Is there anything wrong with that?*

THE LITERARY WORKS OF OU-YANG HSIU
Translated by Ronald Egan
Cambridge University Press
New York, 1984